The Elderberry Bush

Also by Doris Gates

Sarah's Idea
Blue Willow
Sensible Kate
North Fork
River Ranch
Little Vic
The Cat and Mrs. Cary

Illustrated by Lilian Obligado

The Elderberry Bush

by Doris Gates

THE VIKING PRESS   NEW YORK

The poem "Outwitted,"
by Edwin Markham, is reprinted on page 20
by permission of Virgil Markham.

First published in 1967 by The Viking Press, Inc.
625 Madison Avenue, New York, N. Y. 10022
Published simultaneously in Canada by
The Macmillan Company of Canada Limited
Library of Congress catalog card number: 67-20958
Third printing September 1968

Printed in U. S. A. by The Vail-Ballou Press

To my goddaughter

Josephine Jones Ryan

whose grandmother lived some of it

Contents

1   *The Last Day*   9

2   *The Sacajawea Summer*   32

3   *A Visit to Uncle Aaron*   66

4   *Mr. Whipple*   89

5   *Mother Goes to Town*   118

6   *Father Makes Christmas*   143

1

The Last Day

Julie and Elizabeth had finished breakfast and now were in their upstairs bedroom getting ready for the last day of school. Next to Christmas, the Last Day was the best day of the year, since it marked the beginning of summer vacation. Three months without school! Paradise was not to be compared to such bliss. For paradise was pleasantly remote, while the Last Day was joyously here and now. And today, of course, the girls would wear their best dresses and their brand-new patent-leather Mary Jane slippers.

Elizabeth stuck one foot out and wiggled it as she admired the sheen of the black leather. Suddenly she put her foot down.

"Will Ethel Tucker have on shoes today?" she asked Julie.

Elizabeth, who was a year younger than Julie, thought her sister the wisest person in the world next to Father and Mother. And, of course, Clara, who was Father's cousin and had come to help when Elizabeth was born eight years ago. Happily for all the Allens, Clara had stayed on, helping.

Julie was over at the window looking into the top branches of the ash maple growing beside the back steps. Yesterday she *thought* she had seen an oriole's nest there, and now she was leaning out of the window, her face almost touching the wide, flat leaves. She appeared not to have heard her sister.

Elizabeth crossed the room and touched Julie's shoulder. "Will Ethel Tucker have on shoes today?" she asked again.

Though most of the boys had been going barefoot for the past couple of months, none of the girls, except Ethel Tucker, ever did.

Julie drew her head in and considered Elizabeth's question.

From down the hall came Father's voice, singing with fierce energy as he shaved. Though perfectly tuneless, his songs were always well-worth listening to, for, while the first line and the rhythm were always the same, the words varied to fit the occasion. Now, as the two girls wondered about Ethel Tucker, they heard:

"And then he told those children
And those children they did say,
That no more they'd leave their father,
For today was the Last Day."

The phrases of the song came jerkily between strokes of the razor.

When it had ended, Julie said, "Maybe she'll just stay home."

Her words were hardly a direct answer to her sister's question, but Elizabeth understood what she meant. Ethel would stay home because she didn't have shoes for the Last Day.

Ethel had started coming to school only two weeks ago. While there was little to distinguish her from several other girls in Miss White's room, she was distinctly in a class by herself. True, she was a skinny little thing with large blue eyes looking out of a thatch of stringy blond hair. But there were other girls in that room almost as skinny. Several of them rarely had their hair combed. And though she was the only girl who came to school barefooted, this, in itself, would not have been enough to set her apart. Ethel's claim to distinction at Orchard School lay in the fact that she was poor. She was poor among a group of children none of whom was rich. It was suspected that she didn't always have enough to eat. To cap it all, Ethel Tucker had no mother. She was poor indeed.

The Tucker family had established itself in the little shack next to the blacksmith shop a block up the street from the school. This was handy for Mr. Tucker, who worked at the blacksmith shop with Mr. Rogers, the owner. But the house was hardly more than one room and a lean-to, so the six Tuckers must have been badly crowded inside it.

Here Ethel kept house for the four younger children and her father. She did, that is, until a truant officer called at the blacksmith shop one day and insisted that she be allowed to go to school. After that visit, the baby sister was cared for at the Convent of the Holy Names during the school week, and Ethel went to school. Stretching a point, Miss Harvey, principal of Orchard School, allowed little Chester, aged three, to tag along with the other Tuckers. Every morning and afternoon he took a nap in the first-grade cloakroom on two straight chairs shoved together. There his older brother, who was in first grade, could watch over his slumbers and lift him back whenever he rolled off the chairs, as he sometimes did.

Though at first the Tuckers had caused a stir of interest at Orchard School, it wasn't long before everyone was taking them in stride. Ethel's poverty and bare feet came to be accepted, just as Herman Dilling's unquenchable badness had come to be accepted. Every school had at least one bad boy in it; so inevitably, every school had to have some

poor children in it. Ethel Tucker, the poor girl, became at last simply poor Ethel Tucker.

"How will she get her report card if she doesn't
come on the Last Day?" persisted Elizabeth.

"Someone could take it up to the blacksmith
shop," answered Julie. "Miss White would."

Elizabeth nodded, feeling reassured. You could
count on Miss White.

They came out of the bedroom and went down
the long shadowy hall toward the head of the
stairs. At the bathroom door they paused to say,
"Good-by, Father."

Instantly, the door was snatched open and a man
stood on the threshold, peering at them over a
mask of white lather. "Make your poor old father
proud this afternoon. He isn't long for this world."
His voice, issuing through a hole in the mask, was
dolefully solemn.

The girls giggled. A sturdier, healthier man than
Father could hardly be imagined. He had been
talking like this for as long as they could remember.

"You're sure you know your pieces?" he demanded, his dark eyes darting anxiously from one
grinning face to the other. The girls nodded.
"Good!" he cried, turning back into the bathroom
and slamming the door. As Julie and Elizabeth
continued down the hall, another tuneless song followed loudly after them:

"And then he told those children
That their pieces they did know,
And the reason that he told them
Is because they told him so."

Down in the kitchen they stopped for their mother's inspection.

"Let me look at you," she said, as she did every morning.

This morning the inspection was rather prolonged, because, of course, this was the Last Day.

"You look very nice," she said at last. "I shall be proud of you this afternoon."

Like Father, Mother was referring to the parts they were to take in the program.

She gave Elizabeth's hair ribbon a parting twitch, and said to Julie, "Remember, dear, it's not 'thus on its sounding anvil-shape,' but 'thus on its sounding anvil—*shape* each burning deed and thought.' Pause after 'anvil.' "

Julie, who loved horses, had chosen "The Village Blacksmith" for the Last Day. Now she nodded, moving the high lights on her smooth dark bangs.

"I'll remember," she promised.

Elizabeth had chosen "Abou Ben Adhem" because it reminded her of *The Arabian Nights*, a book she loved. She knew the poem perfectly and understood most of it.

They kissed their mother good-by and moved on

through the kitchen to the screened back porch. Clara was there putting a dish of something into the big wooden icebox.

"Got your lunches?" she asked without turning around.

Sometimes they wondered if Clara had eyes in the back of her head. Of course, in all the excitement of the Last Day, they had forgotten to pick up their lunch pails. As they went meekly back into the kitchen they heard Clara's sniff behind them. It could mean almost anything, that sniff. This morning it plainly signified disgust, but the girls felt no concern. Clara always acted terribly afraid that Julie and Elizabeth would guess how much she loved them.

They emerged from the kitchen, each with a big square tobacco can in her hand. The tobacco cans made perfect lunch boxes, for they fastened tightly and had a neat handle on the top. These cans had a pen painted on one side. Father had had to smoke Penn tobacco for quite a while in order to provide his daughters with the brand of lunch box fashionable at Orchard School this year. His duty accomplished, he had gone back to Prince Albert in the small flat cans.

The girls went carefully out the back screen door, swinging it wide and stretching their feet to the second step. Fanny, Father's Irish setter, was sprawled along the top step. The screen door swung safely out over her. Fanny had not the slightest fear that anyone would step on her, because no one ever had. Now, as the children maneuvered past her and down the steps, she thumped her fringed tail lazily a couple of times, sighed mightily, and let them go.

They walked through the fenced kitchen garden to the driveway and down to the county road. Swinging their lunch pails, they started trudging steadily the mile and a half that lay between them and their destination. At the elderberry bush which marked the north boundary of their home place, they turned to wave. Once past the elderberry bush, they would be out of sight of the tall white house and completely on their own. They thought of the bush as a marker between the known and whatever lay beyond. Now, though at some distance, they were still under the eye of the double kitchen windows. They could see their mother's figure at one window and they knew she was waving, though they were too far away to tell. Then another figure appeared at the second of the pair of windows and they knew that Clara was waving too. They waved back, then turned and walked resolutely on past the elderberry bush and out of sight of home.

Julie and Elizabeth, though a year apart, shared the same classroom. Julie, a fourth-grader, sat next

to the windows. Elizabeth was with the third-
graders on the other side of the room. Ethel
Tucker, though the oldest child in the whole room,
sat across the aisle from Elizabeth. Evidently Ethel

had missed a good deal of school during the ten years of her life.

The moment Elizabeth entered the classroom, she saw with dismay that Ethel had not stayed home after all. There she sat behind her desk, her face unusually animated as she watched the children coming in. Had Ethel, too, caught the excitement of the Last Day? For once, her hair was combed. It was neatly parted in the middle and hung in two tight braids fastened each with a rubber band. It wasn't until Elizabeth had taken her seat that she was able to check on Ethel's feet. Today, as on all other days, they were bare. Carefully Elizabeth looked at the other children. As near as she could tell, they all had on shoes. Even Herman Dilling was wearing shoes today. She tried to catch Julie's eye across the room to signal the dreadful news that Ethel Tucker was the only child without shoes on the Last Day. But Julie was already deep in a book and wouldn't look up.

A second row of windows ran along the back of the room, and in the corner where the two rows of windows met, Miss White had her desk.

Miss White had red hair and usually wore a green dress. Sometimes she wore a white blouse under a green jacket. But you could count on Miss White's wearing green. You could count on her for other things, too.

Every day, right after lunch, Miss White read to

the whole room. Everybody was almost good all morning so that Miss White would read to them after lunch. Following the reading, things livened up. Notes found their way up and down the aisles, and here and there a child dared to whisper. Herman Dilling nearly always ended the day standing in the corner. But even Herman was fairly good during the morning.

"Good morning, boys and girls," Miss White greeted them, the tuning fork in one hand and a book open in the other.

"Good morning, Miss White," chorused all the children.

Miss White twanged a note out of the tuning fork, gave it to the children, and all the voices rose in the song with which they began each new school day.

> "Father, we thank Thee for the night,
> And for the pleasant morning bright;
> For rest and food and loving care,
> And all that makes the world so fair."

Then they settled down to work.

"I think we will take time this morning to go over the recitations once more," said Miss White. "Alberta Swall, we start with you."

Alberta rose and minced to the front of the room. She was a rather stout little girl with a wide, blank face, wide vacant gray eyes, and a small demure mouth which she kept folded up like a buttonhole. Now she made a curtsy to the class, at which they all giggled, and, unabashed, began her recitation.

It concerned a heroine named Grace Darling who had rowed across a storm-tossed sea to some shipwrecked people and rescued them. Alberta had learned the piece perfectly, as she learned everything, and she recited it with enthusiasm. In spite of themselves, for no one could really like Alberta, the whole room listened with respect. When she had finished, she curtsied again and sat down to applause that was only partly derisive.

"Are you sure you want to curtsy this afternoon?" Miss White asked her.

"My mother thought it would be more gracious," returned Alberta primly.

"Very well," said Miss White with the faintest trace of a sigh. "Lester Andrews, you're next."

Lester had chosen a short poem about circles. It was just about the shortest poem he could find anywhere. But Miss White liked it so much she said he might learn it if he looked up all the words. The only words Lester hadn't known were *heretic* and *flout*. He had explained them to the class. So now he spoke easily and with conviction.

"He drew a circle that shut me out—
Heretic, rebel, a thing to flout.

But Love and I had the wit to win:
We drew a circle that took him in."

Lester's bony wrists protruded beyond the sleeves of his jacket. Just once he started to put his hands into the pockets of his corduroy knickers, remembered, and drew them back. He looked almost strange to his classmates in his ribbed black stockings and the new shoes with the little tabs sticking out the back of them. And his straw-colored hair had not yet had time to become comfortably rumpled. Intrigued by his unfamiliar appearance, few of the children bothered to listen to what he was saying.

But this morning, for the first time, the poem spoke to Elizabeth. She listened with excitement as the words began to have real meaning for her. A very special meaning. "We drew a circle that took him in."

She glanced across the aisle to where Ethel Tucker sat, one bare foot resting upon the instep of the other.

Quickly Elizabeth reached down a hand and unbuttoned the strap of one Mary Jane pump. Next, she unbuttoned the other. Now for the stockings. While Miss White commented on Lester's recital, Elizabeth dug frantically to free them. She had one off before Miss White said, "Now we'll hear from the third-graders. Elizabeth Allen, will you favor us, please?"

Elizabeth, her face rosy from her struggles, slid off the second stocking and rose. She cast a beseeching eye toward Julie and padded to the front of the room in a perfect stillness. Her eyes were lowered to her white, naked feet, so she missed Julie's shocked eyes, the boys' delighted grins, and Alberta Swall's buttonhole mouth, now a round o of surprise.

In the continuing silence, she began, "Abou Ben Adhem, may his tribe increase . . ." and went on to the end with a throat so dry she wondered that any sound could come out of it. Incredibly, the words tumbled from her in a frantic rush. It seemed as if she merely held her mouth open and they came spilling forth of their own momentum. At last it was over and she was back in her seat, her face scarlet and her heart pounding. What would Miss White say?

"I think, Elizabeth," came the teacher's calm voice from behind the desk in the corner, "I think it would be better if you spoke more slowly this afternoon. You will have a larger audience, remember, and each word must be heard and understood to the very back of the assembly room."

You could count on Miss White!

Two other children were called on and then it was Julie's turn. Elizabeth hadn't dared raise her head since she had finished her recitation. But now she lifted it to look at her sister. And her heart nearly leaped out of her chest. *Julie was barefooted too!*

Again Miss White refused to take note of anything unusual in the Allen sisters' appearance. She even praised Julie for remembering to pause after *anvil.*

With Julie's performance, the recitations came to an end. All the other children in the room were to be bunched with the soloists in a singing of "The Star-Spangled Banner." Miss White's room would perform last and thus the program would conclude on a suitably patriotic note.

So now all the children rose and arranged themselves at the front of the room in the places they would have on the stage. Miss White had put the soloists in the back row, thus equalizing honors for the audience of parents. This placed Ethel Tucker smack in the middle of the front row.

The whole school was seething with excitement when the pupils trooped back to their rooms following the noon recess. The performance would begin at two. But much before that time, the parents would start arriving. And as each automobile or horse-drawn vehicle pulled up in front of the schoolhouse, every head in the classrooms on that side of the building would twist to see who it was.

The Allens would come in the big red Peerless

with the shining brass radiator, because Father would be here today. Only Father could drive the Peerless. Only he had the power in his shoulders to crank it, though even he panted like everything by the time the motor caught and turned on its own power. Sometimes it took a lot of cranking and considerable fiddling with the magneto to accomplish this. Today, unless the magneto failed, the Peerless would be out under the eucalyptus trees.

This certainly gave Elizabeth pause as she sat turning over in her mind the plan which she and Julie had cooked up during their lunch hour. It was nothing less than to leave off their shoes and stockings when their turn came to recite. It was a daring plan and one which they well knew might have serious repercussions. Never in all their lives had they gone barefooted, and to appear so in public might stretch their mother's love and understanding to the breaking point. They felt somewhat less worried about Father. He could nearly always be counted on to see their side of things. But this was different. They had never risked public disgrace before.

Miss White had not appeared after the noon recess. And no one felt any concern, for this was the Last Day. Even Miss White's daily routines might be affected by it. In her absence, an eighth-grade girl was "keeping order," and Herman Dilling was having the time of his life.

With genuine relief, Elizabeth noted that Ethel Tucker, too, had not returned from lunch. Evidently she had wisely decided to stay home. Now the drastic plan which she and Julie had determined upon would not be necessary.

Steadily, fatefully, the Seth Thomas clock on the wall above Miss White's desk ticked off the seconds above the clamor of Herman's clowning and the futile nagging of the eighth-grade girl. By this time there was a long mixed row of automobiles and horse-drawn vehicles under the eucalyptus trees beyond the school grounds. But the big red Peerless was not among them. That magneto again! With Ethel out of the picture, Elizabeth wanted with all her heart to have her family present for the Last Day exercises.

Two o'clock came and still Miss White had not returned.

Occasionally there was the sound of applause from the assembly room upstairs where the upper classes had begun performing. Tension began to mount. Where was Miss White? At last, at half past two, the door opened and there she stood. She looked flushed and a bit harried as she beckoned the children to her. Their time had come! Quietly they slipped out of their seats and toward the door. On tiptoe, she led them across the big hall and up the wide stairs and down another hall past the assembly room to the door which led to the backstage area. And there in the gloom, the first person Elizabeth spied was Ethel Tucker! She hadn't stayed home, after all. She was standing in an almost dark corner and there were several children between her and Elizabeth. But it was Ethel, all right.

The sisters exchanged glances and in the feeble light each read the despair in the other's eyes. They must go through with their plan, magneto or no magneto, and, as one, they bent to undo their stockings.

They watched with hopeless eyes Alberta's and Lester's shadowy outlines as each in turn mounted the short flight of steps to the stage, parted the curtains, and stepped before the audience. In terribly short time they were back with hearty applause ringing behind them. Then it was Elizabeth's turn.

Blindly she pattered toward the steps, unaware of Miss White's desperate attempt to reach her. She stumbled painfully once, but kept resolutely on. Nothing was going to stop her now. Ethel Tucker was not going to be the only child without shoes on the Last Day. Fumbling, she parted the curtains and faced a blur of faces in the bright light from the windows ranging along one side of the assembly room. If she heard the faint gasp which greeted her appearance, she paid it no heed, and stood resolute as a Christian martyr, her naked feet pressed close together.

Faintly she began, "Abou Ben Adhem, may his tribe increase." With those familiar words, the audience swam into focus and Elizabeth recognized three faces gradually emerging from among those on the back row. Father and Mother and Clara had indeed arrived! Mother's face looked shocked, Father's bewildered, and Clara was just delivering herself of a huge sniff. But Elizabeth kept staunchly on until the merciful moment when the poem ended and she could disappear between the stage curtains. The applause behind her was polite, almost questioning.

Coming through the curtains, she bumped into Julie, who stood barefooted and ready to pounce upon the stage the moment Elizabeth left it.

"It's not your turn," Elizabeth whispered. But Julie gave her a shove and stepped into the light.

Elizabeth, wondering, pattered down the stairs to join the others in the gloom of backstage. There, "Under the spreading chestnut tree," came to them in ringing tones.

The waiting children remained utterly still while Julie's voice went confidently on. She even remembered the "anvil—shape" business and spoke the line correctly. You would almost have thought she was wearing shoes!

When at last she had finished and returned to Elizabeth's side, she was tensely quiet. Without a whisper between them, the sisters waited while the last two performers spoke their pieces. Just once Elizabeth asked softly why Julie had gone ahead of turn, but Julie only shook her head and placed a finger on her lips.

Now it was time for the grand finale. All the children started up the stairs to the stage, the ones in the first row going ahead of all the others. Among these was Ethel Tucker. Elizabeth fastened her eyes on the little figure for whom she and Julie had dared so much, and her heart almost turned over. *Ethel Tucker was wearing shoes!*

She turned to Julie, her eyes shocked and questioning.

"Miss White got them for her this noon," whispered Julie. "She told me while you were reciting. That's why I went right after you."

"But you were barefooted, too," said Elizabeth.

Julie nodded as they took their stations in the back row and waited for the curtain to be drawn open. "Miss White tried to stop you, and I was afraid she would try to stop me, so I stayed up by the curtain. I knew she wouldn't make a fuss there. I didn't want you to be the only one."

"Will the whispering in the back row please stop?" said Miss White.

Now the curtain was drawn wide. Sudden, crashing chords shook the scarred old upright piano below the stage as Miss Harvey, working from the shoulders down, sounded the first notes of "The Star-Spangled Banner."

With one upsurging movement, the audience came to its feet. "Oh, say can you see . . ." rang out gloriously from the stage, across the assembled parents, through the windows, and beyond the school grounds. For now the whole audience was singing. Elizabeth thought the song had never sounded so grand.

"Whatever put the idea in your heads?" asked Father.

They were all in the Peerless, whizzing down the road at a good thirty miles an hour. Julie and Elizabeth sat on the wide back seat with Clara between them. Inside them both was a wonderful warm feeling.

Miss White had explained everything and Mother had promised to call a meeting of the Grange ladies at once to take up with them the matter of the Tucker family.

"I just wish," she told Miss White, "that Julie and Elizabeth had said something to me before taking this method of expressing their sympathy for the little Tucker girl. What will people think?"

At this point Father entered the conversation. "As long as my bills are paid, I don't care what people think," he said. "Sometimes it takes something mighty special to make you able to stand in another person's shoes. Or out of 'em," he added with a wink at Julie and Elizabeth.

Now he was asking what had actually put the idea into their heads. For a moment silence followed his question, and then Elizabeth spoke.

"It was a poem," she confessed shyly. "Lester's poem about circles. I wanted to make a circle that took her in."

Nobody said anything more until they were past the elderberry bush and the tall white house had come into sight. Then Father burst into tuneless song:

> "And then he told those children
> That those children can't be beat,
> And he's proud to be their father
> Though there's nothing on their feet."

2

The Sacajawea Summer

It all began with a book from the library.

Every Saturday Mother went into town for books and groceries. If for some reason Father couldn't take her in the Peerless, she went in the buggy behind Old Bess. Very often Clara went with her. If Clara stayed home, then Julie and Elizabeth went. The buggy had only one seat.

The seven miles to town were long as measured by the unhurried clomping of the heavy-footed plow horse, and Mother welcomed company for the drive. The girls liked the slow ride to town behind Old Bess. You could see almost as much as if you were walking, and it was wonderful to have

Mother all to themselves with nothing for her to be busy about except keeping Old Bess to the right side of the road and moving.

Mother had chosen the book especially for Julie and it was about Indians. Among the adventures it described was one involving a young Indian woman named Sacajawea. With her baby strapped to her back, Sacajawea had led an expedition of white men from the Mississippi River all the way across the plains and deserts to the Pacific Ocean. She had been the official scout of the Lewis and Clark Expedition.

The story captured Julie's imagination as nothing else ever had. She would sit, chin on hand, looking off into space dreaming about the Indian guide, wondering what it would be like to have a whole expedition of men dependent on your knowledge of a wide land. She began walking with a lilt in her step, and longed for a pair of moccasins and a fringed shirt.

One day Elizabeth came upon her standing on the roof of the cow barn. She was shielding her eyes with one hand and pointing dramatically into the West with the other. Around her head was a band of cloth which held at the back a single black feather. It was almost tall enough to be an eagle's feather and must once have belonged to a fairly large bird. Elizabeth wondered where Julie had found it.

For a long moment she studied her sister standing atop the cow barn and then she called out, "What are you doing?"

Julie dropped her arm and collapsed onto the ragged shingles as suddenly as if she'd been shot. Her face scarlet, she looked down at Elizabeth from the eaves.

"Promise you won't tell?"

"Of course I won't," said Elizabeth.

"I was playing Sacajawea."

"What's that?"

Julie explained briefly.

"Where did you get that feather?"

"From Gloom, that's where," returned Julie grimly.

Elizabeth's eyes widened with astonishment. "You mean you pulled it out of him yourself?"

Julie nodded, pleased at the note of admiration in her sister's voice. "You bet I did. I tried the roosters first, but they were too scary. Couldn't get near 'em. So it had to be Gloom. I went up and hissed at him and he came waddling right over. But I'm bigger now. This time, when he spread his wings and started for me, I just tackled him. The next thing he knew, I was on one side of the back yard and he was on the other, and I had one of his feathers."

"You wanted it that much," said Elizabeth, marveling.

Gloom was the big Muscovy drake who waddled about the ranch, hissing and threatening every creature that crossed his path. Julie had once made the mistake of hissing back, and Gloom had sailed into her, beating her black and blue. Since that time, she had given him a wide berth. No one could ever understand why Mother insisted on having Muscovies, which hissed and fought—ducks weren't supposed to do either. But then, Mother had a taste for the unusual. "It's why she married me," Father said.

So now Elizabeth was properly impressed to learn that her sister had risked getting close enough to Gloom to remove one of his wing feathers.

"Well," said Julie in response to Elizabeth's remark, "you can't be Sacajawea without a feather. Anyway you can't *feel* like her without one. I know because I tried and it didn't work."

"What does it feel like with a feather?"

Julie took a deep breath and smiled mysteriously. How could she make Elizabeth understand that just moments before this had not been the cow barn? It had been a mighty promontory. Below, where lay the cowyard, and beyond it the henhouse and chicken run, and beyond that the orchard, had spread an undulating land intersected by wide watercourses and rimmed in the vague distance by mountains whose towering summits could only be imagined.

But Elizabeth was awaiting an answer.

"You can't explain it," said Julie.

"Can you play it on the ground?" Elizabeth was a rather timid child.

Julie shook her head. "You have to be high up. You see, Sacajawea had to climb mountains and look out across the land to get her bearings."

Elizabeth nodded understandingly. At the same time, she relinquished all hope of ever coming close to the heart of the Indian guide. The cow barn was by all odds the lowest roof on the ranch and even that was too lofty for Elizabeth.

"Come on down and we'll go find Father," she said. "He's at the engine house."

Julie lowered herself to the ground (the cow-barn roof sloped conveniently, so it was a short drop) and joined her sister. Together they went along the wagon path, each following in a wheel track, until they came to the weathered building that housed the brick furnace, boiler, and engine of the orchard pumping plant. The last irrigation before harvest was finished and Father was draining the water from the boiler pipes.

They came to the wide front door with the high brick wall of the furnace just beyond it and entered. They turned the corner of the furnace and started down the narrow aisle which led to the steam engine. There was Father, tinkering with the belt wheel. He looked up, saw them, and gave a yell. Then he dropped his tools, grabbed his pipe out of his mouth, and dashed out the side door.

"Indians!" he cried. "Indians! We're surrounded!"

Julie had forgotten all about the headband and Gloom's feather. In chagrin she reached for them, hauled them off, and flung them down. Then she and Elizabeth took off after Father.

He was headed between the rows of orchard trees to where Fred, the hired man, was disking down the irrigation ditches.

"Run, Fred, Indians," he screeched, then whirled to peer back at the pursuers through the crotch of a prune tree. But Fred, grinning, kept his eye on the team. The two girls came steadily on, jumping the irrigation ditches when they came to them, and at last they overtook Father.

"Why, I thought you were Indians," he said as they came up to him. "What happened to the feather?"

"I threw it away," said Julie.

"May I ask whom you were impersonating and why?" he said, reaching for his tobacco can.

Julie told him, and he listened as he puffed his pipe into action again.

"How would you like to lead an expedition to the Pacific Ocean?" he asked, his dark eyes earnestly upon her.

"I'd like it," said Julie.

"Then go up to the house and tell your mother that we are leaving for the Pacific Ocean in exactly two days. Tell her there's nothing to do around here for the next two weeks but watch the fruit ripen and feed the stock, and Fred can do both for us. Now scoot along; I want to talk to Fred."

Two days later, with Julie sitting on the front seat of the Peerless, Fanny at her feet, and Mother and Clara and Elizabeth on the back seat, they drove down the driveway and onto the county road and past the elderberry bush and on to the pass in the mountains that would take them to the Pacific Ocean. Father had put the top down so they could view the country better.

He and Julie had gone carefully over the maps of the area, and Julie had chosen to go by way of the Los Gatos Gap because that was the shortest route. Mother protested that the road was high and dangerous, but Father sided with his guide and insisted that the Peerless was equal to the grades and that he'd be very careful on turns.

Mother looked surprised when told that Julie, as guide, would of course ride in the front seat. But she surrendered her place graciously when she learned that Fanny and a five-gallon can of gasoline would also be there.

"Wouldn't want to face the wilderness without a good dog, and there's only one town along the way where you can get gasoline," Father told her.

Luggage was strapped on both running boards of the Peerless and as much was stowed inside as several pairs of feet would allow.

The preparations had been almost as exciting as the trip itself. Father had phoned around among his friends and located a seaside cottage that nobody was using at the moment, and which its owners were delighted to let the Allen family have. So

Father had gone over to pick up the key and get precise directions for finding the place. He even learned about a fisherman friend of the owners named Menzel who had a boat. Then the Allens had to decide on what clothes, books, and provisions to take.

Julie and Elizabeth had been to the ocean only once before in their whole lives and then they were so young as to make the excursion unimportant to their memories. "The coast," as they usually referred to it, was thirty miles away on the other side of the mountains, over winding, rutty, narrow roads which had to be traveled slowly and at some risk, for the turns were sharp and only now and then were there places wide enough to allow two vehicles to pass each other.

On this day, when they were deep in The Gap, suddenly, above the roar of the gears, they caught a new sound. It had a bell-like quality and over it rose the shouts of a man. Fanny got to her haunches, pricked up her ears, and whined.

"Mule team coming," announced Father.

"Harry, what will we do?" asked Mother nervously.

They were climbing along a very narrow stretch of road, with a deep canyon on one side and a high cliff on the other.

"We'll manage," said Father a little grimly. "Just keep your shirts on."

"I'm getting out," said Clara firmly, reaching for the door.

"Well, I'm not stopping on this grade to let you," said Father.

"You won't have to stop," said Clara. "I can make it all right."

And indeed it seemed as if the Peerless was barely moving as it labored up, up the steep grade. Clara opened the door and hopped to the ground, and the Peerless pulled ahead of her. Elizabeth turned and watched Clara plodding behind them until the car rounded a curve and they lost sight of her.

"Will she ever catch up with us?" asked Elizabeth. It seemed awful that Clara should be abandoned here on the mountainside.

"Hush," said Mother, anxiety making her irritable.

"But will she?" persisted Elizabeth.

"Of course," said Mother. "Your father will turn off the first chance he gets, and we'll wait for Clara while the mule team goes by."

And that's just what happened. Around the next bend, the road leveled out a bit and there, under some redwoods, was a space quite large enough to accommodate the Peerless. Father pulled into it and stopped. He turned off the motor. Now the sound of bells filled the air and soon they heard the creak of cart wheels and the screech of brakes, along with the shouts of the driver. The leaders of the team swung into sight and then the girls saw that each of them wore atop its collar a metal framework holding a row of bells. At every movement of the mules' heads, the frames moved and the bells inside them set up a pleasant jangling. This was, of course, to warn other vehicles that a mule team was coming.

Julie and Elizabeth watched with wide eyes as the team, ten mules harnessed in pairs, came abreast of them. They were pulling a high load of oak wood. The driver was managing the team with one line fastened to the head of one of the leaders.

He stopped the team and called down from his lofty seat to the family in the car. "Ain't you got a better place to ride than this?" He laughed heartily at his own joke.

"We're going to the coast," Father informed him. "Any teams behind you?"

"One more following," said the driver. " 'Bout a mile back. Better wait here till he's passed."

"I will," said Father. "How far to the summit?"

" 'Bout three miles. Ain't you never been over this way before?"

"Been a few years," said Father.

The driver looked down at them and chewed his tobacco thoughtfully for a moment, then spat over the side, and said, "I guess that there automobile is up to it."

"I think so," said Father with only a trace of pride.

"But when it comes to real loads, it takes a mule," opined the driver. "Ain't never goin' to see one of them fancy engines pullin' loads over these mountains!"

Before Father could refute this, as he most certainly would have, the driver yelled to his leaders, and the team pulled by, the brakes screeching as they held the heavy load.

While the four in the Peerless waited for the second team to pass, Clara caught up with them and got into the car.

"Did the walk settle your nerves?" asked Father solicitously.

Clara only sniffed.

After a long, grinding pull, they topped the summit and again Father stopped the car. "Climb down, Sacajawea," he ordered, getting out of the car. He opened a back door. "You too," he said to the three sitting there. Already Fanny was out, circling and barking in high excitement.

Father led them to where they could look out to the horizon and then they all exclaimed at what they saw—all but Elizabeth. Far, far in front of them was a line of dark blue.

"The Pacific Ocean!" announced Father, as if he had arranged for it to be there.

"Where are the waves?" asked Elizabeth, feeling considerably let down. This was nothing like the pictures she had seen of oceans. Where were the tossing waves, the lowering clouds, the ship in distress, the lifeboat struggling through the first line of breakers? This streak of blue was tame indeed.

"We're too far away to see the waves," Mother explained. "They are there, all right."

"And be sure you stay out of them," said Clara, "except when there's a grownup with you."

Father looked at her and grinned. "Do you intend to abide by that rule too, Clara?"

Clara sniffed and returned to the car.

Mother looked annoyed. "You shouldn't tease her," she scolded. "You know she's timid."

"She always was," said Father, referring to those far-off days when he and Clara had been children together. "Time she got over it."

"It's time you got over teasing her about it, too," said Mother, sticking up for Clara.

Julie and Elizabeth, listening while they studied the horizon, let the words go in one ear and out the other. They loved Clara with unalterable devotion, timid or not, and they knew their parents loved her and that she loved them. Everybody had a weak spot somewhere, as Father often said. Clara's was timidity, and it was the only one they had ever

discovered in her. It caused no one discomfort or
inconvenience except Clara herself. If you had to
have a weak spot, that was the kind of one to
have.

They found the cottage they were to occupy
after only three stops to ask the way. The man at
the grocery store told them in which part of the
village they would find it. A boy on a bicycle told
them how to find the street it was on when they got
to their part of town. And a woman in the house on
the corner told them which house was theirs.

They could hardly believe their good luck when
at last they saw it. A big pine tree stood guard over
the front yard. The back door had a trellis with a
heliotrope vine growing on it and the air all around
was heavy with its perfume. On entering, they discovered that besides a living room and a kitchen,
there was a bedroom downstairs. Upstairs, tucked
under the ridge of the roof which sloped sharply
above it, was one huge bedroom covering the
whole house. It had four double beds in it, so there
was plenty of room for everyone. Clara took the
downstairs bedroom, while Father and Mother and
the two girls took over the upstairs. Mother and
Clara made up the beds first thing while Father
and the two girls unpacked all the kitchen supplies.
This was an easy job, as Mother had given them
strict orders to put nothing into the cupboards. So

it meant just lifting packages and paper bags from their boxes onto the kitchen table and sink.

When they had finished with the beds, Mother and Clara came straight to the kitchen and put away the supplies; then it was time for a snack. Father meanwhile had gone out to chop some kindling and look into the wood supply. Mother would need both to cook supper.

After finishing their sandwiches, and with the house in good order, they started for the beach, Fanny circling excitedly around them. The closer they got to it, the louder grew the sound of the ocean and the stronger came its salt smell, borne to them on the same wind that seemed to be blowing the gulls about the sky. Father began to walk faster, and Julie and Elizabeth kept right beside him. In no time at all, they had left Mother and Clara far behind. Now they could see the waves. Elizabeth began to feel better. This was more like it, she decided as she studied the crashing lines of water critically. Yes, they looked almost like the pictures. Soon they were walking onto the wharf, Father's heels making a hollow sound as he strode along, a trail of tobacco smoke drifting past one shoulder. Halfway to the end, he crossed over to one side. Julie and Elizabeth followed him. As they neared the edge, he turned his head.

"You kids stay back," he said. Then he took

hold of a rope hanging from somewhere above him and called down, "Know anyone here by the name of Menzel?"

"My name's Menzel," came the answer from somewhere under the wharf.

Father let go of the rope, took a few steps along the side of the wharf, and then, apparently stepping off into space, disappeared from sight.

This was too much for the girls. With one move they were at the wharf's edge, peering down in horror. But everything was all right, after all. Father was standing on a kind of raft tied to the piles of the wharf. A flight of stairs led down to the raft, or float, as it was actually called. Father was talking to the man named Menzel, who was standing in the middle of a boat looking unhappily at its motionless engine.

Julie called out, "May we come down?"

"No," said Father without looking up.

"May we sit on the edge and watch?" inquired Elizabeth.

Father glanced up at them briefly and returned his gaze to the boat. "If you don't fall off, you can," he said.

So the girls cautiously seated themselves on the wharf planks and, with their feet hanging over the edge, watched the proceedings below them.

They saw Father make some gestures toward the engine and say something to which Mr. Menzel listened carefully. Next they saw him step from the float into the boat. He went straight to the engine and began tinkering with it.

By the time Mother and Clara came along, Father was up to his elbows in grease and the engine had coughed twice.

"You should have your old clothes on for that, Harry," Mother called down to him.

Father looked up and grinned sheepishly. "This is Mr. Menzel," he called back to her. "My wife, Mrs. Allen," he added, and Mr. Menzel took off his greasy cap and smiled. "My cousin, Miss Allen," he continued, and Mr. Menzel smiled again at Clara, who bowed stiffly. "I'll have this going before long," Father announced to the watching ladies. "Carburetor's plugged."

Mother and Clara drew back and started sauntering on to where a few men and small boys were fishing at the end of the wharf.

"Want to come with us?" Clara asked the girls as she turned away from the float.

They shook their heads and Clara sniffed. "With all there is to see around here, I can't imagine why you want to sit there looking down into a messy boat."

Julie and Elizabeth didn't attempt to explain. Father was down there and so they would remain patiently up here. It was as simple as that.

Mother and Clara had returned from the end of

the wharf and walked the whole distance back to land before a series of engine coughs at last settled down into a noisy and confident chugging. Mr. Menzel looked very pleased.

"Let's try her out," he shouted to Father.

Above, on the wharf, the two watching figures stiffened slightly.

They watched more tensely as Father said something to Mr. Menzel and they saw Mr. Menzel look up and nod quickly. Then above the noise of the engine, Father called up to the girls.

"Listen carefully. Don't budge until I've finished what I'm going to say." Two heads bobbed at him in unison. "We are going to try out the engine and Mr. Menzel has kindly consented to take you along. I want you to slide back from the edge until the heels of your shoes are on the wharf. Then get to your feet and come down those stairs"—he motioned—"*slowly*. I'll tell you what to do when you get down here."

Obediently the girls began sliding backward until their heels rested on the wharf. This put them a good safe distance from the edge and they got to their feet. Walking only a little under a run, they reached the head of the stairs and started slowly down. They arrived at the float and stood waiting for the next command. The ocean swells were causing the float to rise and fall. The boat was rising and falling, too, but somehow the two never seemed to be doing either one at just the same instant. Mr. Menzel and Father leaned over the side of the boat with their arms extended toward the girls.

"Take hold of our hands," said Father, "and when I say 'Jump,' you jump no matter how you may feel about it. Savvy?"

"Yes," they answered, taking hold of the men's hands.

For an instant, the four stood there holding hands and then Father said, "Jump!" The girls jumped as if triggered, and felt themselves swung up and over. The next thing they knew there they were in the boat with the sea looking bigger than it had at any time so far.

Elizabeth let her eye measure the boat's length. It was not a rowboat, of course, and the seats, like benches, were along the sides instead of across. But despite these differences, it looked quite a bit like the lifeboats she had seen being launched in pictures. It seemed very small compared with the wide ocean stretching beyond it.

"Sit down," commanded Father, and they sat.

Now the ocean was almost on a level with their bottoms. It heaved below them, darkly green and immensely deep. Their eyes could penetrate into that deepness only a very little way.

Suddenly a whiteness began floating up through the water toward them. It was about one foot across and its edges seemed to wrinkle in, then wrinkle out again.

"Look!" cried Julie, pointing downward.

Father glanced over the side. "Jellyfish," he announced and immediately turned back to the boat.

Mr. Menzel threw off the rope that held them to the float and they headed out into the bay. Elizabeth reached behind her with both hands to seize the boat's rail. Her eyes were wide with apprehension. But Julie had squirmed around to face the bow, a grin on her face. Sacajawea must have felt like this that day on the Missouri when the boat almost capsized and only her courage and quick thinking had saved the expedition's papers from being swept away!

Julie watched the boat's prow splitting the water and was reminded of the plow furrowing the orchard ground at home. Sometimes a little burst of spray was blown back against her cheek.

They circled the bay, waving once to the two figures moving along the beach with a smaller figure racing ahead of them. It must be Mother and Clara with Fanny. Gulls followed in the wake of the boat, making creaky noises like rusty hinges. But there was nothing suggesting rustiness in their smooth and effortless soaring.

At last they were back at the wharf. Mr. Menzel tied up the boat, and Father stepped onto the float. Then the whole business of hand-holding and jumping began again, only this time in reverse, and the girls were safely unloaded. Father waited long enough to make arrangements to go fishing the next day with Mr. Menzel and then the three Allens climbed the steps to the wharf.

That night Julie lay quietly in bed, going over in her mind all the many excitements of the day. Elizabeth was deeply asleep beside her. Across the room in the soft glow of the coal-oil lamp, Father was reading. Mother, like Elizabeth, was asleep. Over their heads, the roof with its beams and shingles sloped down almost to the floor. It gave a snug feeling to the room. Julie reached up an arm to touch the beam over her head.

What a lot had happened in the last few days! Had it really all started with that book about Sacajawea? Suppose Elizabeth hadn't come along that morning and found her on the cow-barn roof wearing one of Gloom's feathers? Would they all be here now in this house beside the sea? Had Father been intending to come here all along, or had he got the idea when he thought about Sacajawea? You never could tell about Father. Anyway, two lovely, promising weeks lay ahead of them: fourteen days filled with a kind of wonder and adventure she had never known before.

Fanny had stretched herself flat alongside Father's bed and was sound asleep. Now and then her feet jerked and she whimpered in her sleep.

Father looked up from his book and smiled across at Julie. "She's still chasing sea gulls," he whispered. Then he looked sharply at his daughter. "Why aren't you asleep?"

"I don't know," Julie whispered back.

"Well, go to sleep," he said, turning again to his book.

So Julie did.

The next day Father went fishing and Julie came down with the mumps. She woke up with a throat so sore she could hardly swallow.

"Tonsillitis," said Mother and made her gargle with a strong solution of salt water. But though this hurt like fury, it did no good at all. Then a strange soreness began to develop behind Julie's ears. "Mumps," said Mother and put her right back into bed. Clara went for the doctor.

Elizabeth, who had had the mumps in the spring, now mourned for poor unlucky Julie. "Why did you have to wait and get them while we were at the coast?" she wailed. Julie, who hadn't waited intentionally at all, began to sniffle with self-pity. This made her jaws hurt worse than ever.

By the time Father came home with a gunny sack half full of fish, Julie's face was double its normal size, and she could hardly open her mouth. He stood beside her bed looking down into her poor swollen face. "It's a tough break, Sacajawea," he said, "but you'll be all right in a week."

Tears started running out the corners of Julie's eyes. A whole week! Half the vacation! And it would be donkey's years before they got over here again! She could hardly bear her bad luck. Besides, she *hurt!* Of course Elizabeth had suffered too, she reminded herself. But Elizabeth had been lucky. She'd been able to stay a week out of school. She hadn't had to miss half the fun of being at the coast. Julie was feeling very sorry for herself.

Father sat down on the edge of the bed, took her hot hand, and squeezed it comfortingly.

"When I was down on the Amazon," he began, "I had the mumps once."

Julie turned her face to the wall; she wasn't in a mood for one of Father's Amazon stories just now. But Father went right on, perhaps because Elizabeth was also listening, an anticipatory smile on her face.

"My face swelled up so big I couldn't pass between the forest trees and had to sit on a log in the middle of the Amazon River. The way my face was blown up, I thought it might be a year or two before the swelling went down and I was wondering how I'd get anything to eat. Right then, I saw a bump in the river. The bump was swimming toward me, and the next thing I knew two huge jaws had opened up in front of me and those jaws, top

and bottom, were lined with the biggest teeth you ever saw."

Julie's face had turned back from the wall.

"What was it?" asked Elizabeth.

"A crocodile," cried Father. "Right there in the middle of the Amazon, sitting on my log, I was looking down the throat of a crocodile."

"What did you do?" asked Elizabeth, playing the game according to the rules.

"Well, sir, quicker than you can say 'scat,' I reached out and grabbed a jaw with each hand and pulled that crocodile up to the log. Then I braced myself and began forcing the jaws farther apart. The crocodile thrashed around something awful. At times his whole body came clean out of the water. But I held on and the next thing you know I turned him inside out."

He paused to tamp the tobacco down into his pipe before continuing. Then he reached again for Julie's hand and went on with the story.

"Of course my hands were covered with crocodile juice and before I thought to wash them off in the river, I stood there on my log looking at the dead crocodile and sort of running my hands over my face."

He looked down at Julie, whose eyes were as wide as the mumps would allow, and full of wonder.

"The next thing you know, the swelling began to go out of my face. In no time at all I was back to normal. It was the crocodile juice that did it."

He got to his feet. "Come on, Betts," he said to Elizabeth, "we're going to find some crocodile juice for Julie."

Every day thereafter until Julie's mumps were gone, she looked forward to the crocodile juice. Sometimes it was ice cream; sometimes it was soda pop, which she sipped through a straw. Sometimes it was a chocolate bar made very thin, which slipped comfortably between her teeth. These were things that Julie did not have every day and they

were a great treat. But best of all about the crocodile juice, a present came with it.

"That crocodile left me his skin, didn't he?" said
Father. "I don't think the juice would work unless
something enduring came with it."

The first present was a little bisque doll, hardly
taller than Julie's forefinger. She had real hair and
a blue dress and Mary Jane slippers painted on her
feet.

"They have some dress goods down at the store,"
said Mother. "I'll help you make her some other
clothes."

The next present was two small goldfish swim-
ming in a glass globe.

"How will we ever get them home?" asked
Mother.

"They're a proper souvenir of the coast," said
Father, adding, "in a fruit jar."

The crocodile juice not only eased Julie's suffer-
ing; it comforted Elizabeth too. Now she could
have a good time and know that Julie was not
altogether left out.

Mother and Clara took turns staying home with
the invalid. Now and then Father sent the two
ladies off together and sat with Julie. But mostly he
went fishing. Elizabeth hardly stayed home at all.
It wasn't expected that she should. So every day
she went to the beach with Mother or Clara.

It was more fun with Clara, because Clara was

afraid of the water and so was Elizabeth. Mother could swim a steady, reliable breast stroke, which she wanted to teach to her daughter. But Elizabeth preferred to play cautiously in the white water which came curling up the beach after a wave broke. She would stand braced against the undertow, enjoying the tickling of the sand as the receding waters washed it out from under her feet.

A thick, sturdy rope led from the sand right out into the water beyond the breakers, put there for people who couldn't swim. Clinging to the rope, they could work their way along it to the deeper water behind the breakers. There they clung, women and children for the most part, lifted squealing off their feet by the great swells, kicking joyously as the water buoyed them up. Elizabeth watched their fun without the slightest urge to share it, though she did admire the bright swim caps wetly shining like huge beads along the rope.

One wonderful day she went with Father and Mother to the big town a few miles around the bay from their own village. This place had a real business district and streetcars. But best of all, it had a Boardwalk along its beach. The Boardwalk was very wide, so that hundreds of people could saunter there. On its land side were booths, one against another. Here were shooting galleries, a "tunnel of love," shops, and freaks. At one end of the Boardwalk, where it ran off into the sand, was a roller coaster which climbed so high into the sky that Elizabeth knew immediately she wanted no part of it.

The crowds of happy, slow-strolling vacationers proceeded along the walk in two streams which met and passed each other without bumping or confusion. When someone saw a friend and stopped to chat, the crowd simply divided good-naturedly and walked around them. Beyond the Boardwalk, on the ocean side, gaily colored umbrellas with legs sticking out from under them dotted the beach. Everywhere there were people laughing and calling to their children above the roar of the roller coaster and the crashing of the waves.

Halfway along the Boardwalk, exactly opposite the bandstand, was the Arcade. Here Father left Mother and Elizabeth. But first he put five pennies into Elizabeth's hand.

"I'll be back in a minute," he said. "Enjoy yourself."

The Arcade was a big building with not many people in it. Away off across from where Mother and Elizabeth were standing, a man was drawing the picture of a girl who sat in front of him. A few people had gathered around the artist, watching as he applied first one colored chalk then another to the paper pinned to his easel.

"Come," said Mother. "Don't you want to see the moving pictures?"

Elizabeth followed her across the Arcade to one of several large boxes set up on legs. On top of each big box there was a smaller box shaped very much like the stereoscope viewer at home. Elizabeth fitted her face into this viewer, dropped a penny into a slot as Mother directed, then began slowly to turn the crank on the side of the big box. Instantly a light came on and then she saw a picture. Against a black drapery stood a very beautiful young lady in a white ballet skirt. As Elizabeth cranked and peered, the beautiful lady came to life and began to dance. Here was magic, pure magic. Like a fairy tale coming to life, the little dancer leaped and pirouetted on the very tips of her shiny slippers. Elizabeth could hardly breathe from excitement. Then, just when she was beginning to recover from the first shock of the enchantment, the picture became dark. The little dancer was gone.

She withdrew her face from the viewer and looked at Mother.

"Did you like it?" asked Mother, smiling at the wonder in her small daughter's eyes.

"Oh, yes," whispered Elizabeth.

"Then put in another penny," said Mother. "You have four more, you know."

By the time Father returned, Elizabeth had

spent all her pennies on the little dancer and knew what she wanted to do when she grew up.

"What have you there?" asked Mother, nodding at the box Father had tucked under one arm.

"Crocodile juice," he replied, and that was all he would tell her.

They had lunch right there on the Boardwalk, eating something new and delicious called "hot dogs." Anyway, that's what the sign said and Elizabeth, reading it, decided at first she would prefer to eat somewhere else.

Father laughed. "You don't suppose they're serving up real dogs, now do you, Betts?"

Mother explained, "They're frankfurters, Elizabeth, served inside a finger roll with mustard. You'll like them."

And Elizabeth did.

When they got home, they found Julie and Clara sitting in the back yard beside the heliotrope vine. The strong sun had drawn the perfume from its purple blossoms and the still air was saturated with it.

Julie looked excited and happy. "Guess what?" she called as soon as she caught sight of them coming up the garden walk.

"What?" called Father right back.

"The doctor came while you were gone and he says I am all well and can go to the beach tomorrow!"

"I had a feeling that's what he'd say," said Father. "Here's the last of the crocodile juice." And he laid the box on Julie's lap.

As if sensing that this might be a very special moment in her life, Julie looked from Father to Mother and then down at the box.

"Open it!" cried Elizabeth.

Julie untied the string and tipped up the lid. For a moment she just sat there, staring down in astonishment.

"Well," said Father, "aren't you going to take them out?"

Slowly Julie lifted up a pair of moccasins, her two hands fitted into the toes. Then she slid them off her hands and reached again into the box. This time she lifted out a leather shirt. It had beading on the front and was fringed along each arm and around the bottom.

"Oh, Father!" cried Julie.

Everyone looked perfectly delighted with this last of the crocodile juice, everyone except Mother, who had a little worry line between her eyes.

"Shouldn't you have waited until Christmas, Harry?" she asked.

"No," said Father. "There is a tide in the affairs of men. This is the fringed-shirt tide."

While he was speaking, Julie had got out of the chair and was putting on the shirt. It fitted perfectly. Next she unlaced her shoes and slipped her feet into the moccasins. They too were just right. Then she hurled herself into Father's arms, hugging him with all her might. When she had released him, she turned and saw Elizabeth watching her with eyes as shining as her own. Some of the light went out of Julie's.

"Elizabeth didn't have all this fun when she had mumps," she said.

"She's been having fun while you were laid up," said Father. "She hasn't told you all she's been doing because she didn't want to make you feel worse than you already did. Isn't that right, Betts?"

Elizabeth nodded, so Julie felt free to enjoy everything.

At the end of another week of playing in the breakers, of building sand castles, and of eating waffles baked in a tiny shop on the edge of the beach, it was time to return to the ranch.

All the bundles and boxes and bags were put back into the Peerless and once again Julie took her place on the front seat as guide. This time she was wearing a fringed leather shirt and moccasins. And though no headband and feather adorned her dark head, she was Sacajawea to her very bones.

3

A Visit to
Uncle Aaron

Summer was almost over. The harvest would begin
soon, and so would school.

"We must call on Uncle Aaron," announced Father.

"Oh, dear," said Mother. "When?"

She and Clara were right in the middle of making blackberry preserves. Two rows of pint jars
stood on the kitchen table and a big kettle was
bubbling on the range. It was hot in the kitchen.

It had been hot the day before, when they had
gone across Guadalupe Creek to Mr. Whipple's for
the blackberries. He had stopped in one day to say

that the berries were ripe and that the Allens were welcome to all they could pick.

Mother and Clara, with Julie and Elizabeth, had walked over to the berry patch, each carrying a big kettle. Mother and Clara wore old straw hats and had pulled old black cotton stockings up their arms to protect themselves from the thorns of the black-berry bushes. The girls did not have stockings on their arms, because it wasn't expected that they would pick long enough to make cutting the feet off two more pairs worth while. As it was, they picked long enough to get their fill of the good ripe berries and then they left the patch to wander in the creek.

The spell of hot weather had almost dried up the creek. Only a few pools were left around the roots of the sycamores. They found some tiny fish swim-ming languidly in the dingy depths. It would have been easy to catch them, but the girls didn't try. It seemed unfair to take advantage of the poor things struggling to stay alive in the stagnating waters.

"We haven't been to see Uncle Aaron all sum-mer," explained Father, a little defensively, "and once the harvest starts, we won't have another chance for a good long while."

Julie and Elizabeth, who had come into the kitchen in time to hear Father's opening remark, exchanged glances.

"Will we have to go?" asked Julie.

"What a question!" scoffed Mother, scowling into the bubbling berry kettle. "Of course you'll go."

"When?" asked Elizabeth in a small, dispirited voice.

"Ask your father," returned Mother, stirring furiously.

"Tomorrow afternoon," said Father, and Clara sniffed.

"Don't worry about the berries, Alice," she said to Mother. "I'll finish them."

Mother turned from the stove, the stained wooden stirring spoon in her hand. "You'll go with us, of course," she said to Clara.

"I'd rather finish the berries."

"But what would Uncle Aaron think? He's just as much your uncle as Harry's," Mother reminded her.

Uncle Aaron was the brother of Father's father and of Clara's father, both of whom were dead. It was nothing short of miraculous that Uncle Aaron wasn't dead, too, for he was past ninety years old. He had a long white beard and penetrating blue eyes which had never known glasses and with which he scanned the newspaper every morning from front to back, including the classified ads, not missing a single item. He always sat in the same chair in the bay window of the back parlor and if anyone spoke to him while he was reading his paper, he would lower it slightly and snarl at them over its top. He was very rich and he thought he was very wise. Everyone avoided him as much as possible.

His wife, who was Aunt Harriet and only seventy, couldn't avoid him. Nor could his two old-maid daughters. And this had left a mark upon all three of them. Aunt Harriet was a gentle, almost cringing creature with a worn expression and a sweet, apologetic smile. Cousin Hester was strict and unyielding. Cousin Ruby, though no less formal in her manner, was a trace less formidable than her older sister. It was generally conceded outside of Uncle Aaron's household that if Ruby could escape soon, there might be hope for her. But to Julie and Elizabeth neither of the sisters seemed quite human and they were determined never to be anything remotely like them.

"He's a very old man," Father went on, "and the titular head of the family. I don't like him any better than you do, but if for no other reason, we must pay him our duty out of respect for Father's memory." He was, of course, referring to Julie and Elizabeth's dead grandfather. "We haven't been there since last New Year's; it won't hurt any of us to go tomorrow."

Clara sniffed again, but didn't say anything, and it was understood by all present that she would be with the rest of the family when the Peerless headed up the county road past the elderberry bush.

The next day, as the jig-sawed overhang ornamenting the high gables of Uncle Aaron's roof came into view above the orchard trees, Father put on a burst of speed and drew up with a flourish beside the white picket fence. He stopped in a cloud of dust with a screech of brakes that drew the instant attention of the old gentleman seated in the bay window protruding out from the east side of the house. Uncle Aaron was at his usual post.

Now Julie and Elizabeth, stepping down from the car, saw him turn his head with its long white beard. They knew he was roaring for Aunt Harriet or one of "the girls" to go and open the front door.

Cousin Hester and Cousin Ruby were usually referred to as "the Allen girls." Julie and Elizabeth considered the title perfectly ridiculous, for they knew as well as anyone that "the girls" were almost forty, and hence, quite old ladies.

Before Father had time to twist the big round doorbell, the front door opened and there stood Cousin Hester.

"Why, Harry, what a pleasant surprise," she said with a formal smile, stepping back to let them enter. "Alice, you're looking well. How do you do, Clara?"

Julie and Elizabeth brought up the rear.

"How you girls have grown!" declared Cousin Hester, just as she had last New Year's.

They trooped down the hall and into the back parlor, which was separated from the front parlor by sliding doors.

"Well, Harry," said Uncle Aaron from his chair in the bay window. He extended a hand, not bothering to get up, for though he was quite able to do so, one is allowed certain privileges when one is ninety. Father shook the old man's hand, then gave it to Mother. "Alice, you're looking very fit." He merely nodded to Clara, and then his eyes fell on the two little girls.

For a moment he studied them; then he pointed a finger at Julie. "Who are you?" he demanded.

Aunt Harriet had by this time come into the room and now she hurried forward and put an arm around both the girls, hugging them to her thin old sides.

"This is Julie, Father," she informed the old tyrant. "And this is Elizabeth."

She bent and bestowed a light kiss on each of them while Uncle Aaron watched her closely out of his shrewd blue eyes.

Suddenly he reached out a hand toward Elizabeth. She was looking particularly fetching that day in the light-green gingham dress Mother had made for her with white rickrack trimming on its round collar. Her curls had loosened about her face, framing it prettily under her green hair ribbon.

"Come over here and give your old uncle a kiss," demanded Uncle Aaron.

Elizabeth recoiled from that pointing finger, and her cheeks lost some of their bright color. Kiss Uncle Aaron! She raised shocked eyes to Father. Did she really have to plant a kiss on that bearded face?

In all the times they had called on Uncle Aaron, this emergency had never arisen. Both she and Julie had been deeply thankful for the fact that he had never paid the least attention to either one of them. During their visits, which were short out of deference to Uncle Aaron's great age, they merely sat stoically while their eyes roved around the room, centering finally on the mantel, which held an accumulation of unusual objects including a stuffed canary under glass.

Father cleared his throat. "Elizabeth showed signs this morning of a slight cold, Uncle," he fibbed in an effort to spare his daughter. "Better not risk it."

Uncle Aaron growled. He disliked advice, even for his own good. "I haven't lived this long without being exposed to colds. And I ain't going to live so much longer that I need to fear 'em. Come over here, lassie."

Elizabeth went. Gravely the old man leaned to-

ward her while all the rest looked on, and unhesi-
tatingly Elizabeth bent toward him and placed a
kiss squarely in the center of his hairy mouth.

Following that kiss, Elizabeth took a quick step

back from Uncle Aaron and just then, the sliding doors to the front parlor opened and Cousin Ruby walked in. There were greetings and handshakings all over again and Cousin Ruby said, "How you girls have grown!" She turned, explaining to Mother her tardy arrival. "I was cleaning the paint off my hands."

"Paint?" cried Mother. "Are you painting the parlor?"

It was unthinkable that Cousin Ruby and Cousin Hester should be employing themselves in such vulgar fashion. Other women might paint parlors, but never these two.

Cousin Ruby laughed in a deprecating way as she took a seat. "Well, hardly," she said, and Clara, who had helped Mother paint the kitchen only last spring, sniffed. "I am working in oils." She looked down modestly as she made the declaration, smoothing the lap of her dress.

Uncle Aaron began to twitch about in his chair, and Aunt Harriet looked at him uneasily. Cousin Hester rose suddenly and went toward the kitchen, her long serge skirt snapping about her ankles.

"Lot of tomfoolery," growled Uncle Aaron. "Wasting my money on paints and canvas. All she can do is daub."

Julie and Elizabeth looked hastily at each other and then at poor Cousin Ruby. But the cruel words hadn't seemed to affect her at all. She still sat smoothing her lap, a faint smile on her lips. Perhaps she was used to Uncle Aaron.

"Have you taken lessons?" asked Mother hurriedly.

"I've been studying with Mr. Renfrow," murmured Cousin Ruby, a rich color coming into her cheeks.

Father noticed the color and a corner of his mouth twitched. "Aren't you going to let us see them, Ruby?" he asked.

Without a word, she rose and opened the sliding doors. Everyone followed her into the front parlor except Uncle Aaron, who remained in his chair by the window, fidgeting and growling.

Cousin Ruby had been busy, all right. Paintings, some of them in frames, were propped on nearly every chair and sofa in the front parlor. Near the front window, but safely back from the lace curtains, stood her easel. All the paintings were of female figures either seated or standing. All of them were richly, even intricately, clothed in gowns of the current fashion, with something slightly novel added—a ribbon here, a flower there, a new draping of a shoulder or bodice. Hands were not in evidence, being either hidden under a skirt fold or just happening to have slipped over the back of the chair supporting the figure's elegantly clothed arm. Each design was done with utter accuracy and done astonishingly well.

However, there was one glaring peculiarity to each of the paintings. Not one of them had a face. Where the face should have been, at the end of the neck and under the hairdo, there was simply blank canvas.

"Ruby, you have real talent," said Mother firmly.

"Mr. Renfrow thinks so," admitted Ruby modestly.

"You can really tell what kind of cloth it is," said Clara, peering closely at two canvasses set side by side on a horsehair sofa. "This one is velvet and this one is satin. It's plain as day. I don't see how you do it."

Cousin Ruby looked pleased, but a roar issued from the back parlor. "Ask her how much of that work was done by Renfrow. He spends almost as much time in that front parlor as she does."

Cousin Ruby colored again. "The designs are mine," she said. "Mr. Renfrow helps me occasionally with the draping and texturing. Of course I can't do faces yet," she finished.

"And neither can Renfrow," growled a voice behind them. Uncle Aaron had entered the front parlor. "It's all ridiculous, I say. A woman your age cooped up here three times a week with that little nincompoop of a fortune hunter."

"Oh, Father," gasped Cousin Ruby.

But Mother, outraged, stepped squarely in front

of Uncle Aaron. "You're not being fair to Ruby, Uncle," she informed him, her eyes blazing. "These paintings show a lot of talent. Ruby could be a dress designer, given half a chance."

It wasn't often anyone ever spoke up to Uncle Aaron and now Julie and Elizabeth watched tensely for the effect of Mother's words. But, strangely, the old man reached out and slipped a hand under her arm.

"If she's got to paint, why don't she paint sumpin' pretty, like the barn?" His tone was almost conciliatory.

"Because Ruby isn't interested in barns, that's why," returned Mother staunchly. "She's interested in clothes."

"Huh," grunted Uncle Aaron, turning slowly toward the back parlor and drawing Mother along with him. "If you ask me, she's interested in that nincompoop, Renfrow."

"If you ask me," declared Father, catching fire from Mother, "it's about time the girls got interested in somebody."

Uncle Aaron paused and turned again to beam the full force of his penetrating stare onto Father. "Who'd take care of me in my old age?" he whined, leaving Father helpless to reply.

Julie and Elizabeth remained in the parlor after the grownups had withdrawn. They were aware that the sliding doors had been shut behind them, but they still stood, lost in contemplation of Cousin Ruby's paintings.

"What was it like, kissing him?" asked Julie at last.

Elizabeth giggled. "About like kissing Fanny."

Julie doubled up in silent mirth at this, and Elizabeth clapped her hands over her mouth in an effort to hold back her laughter at the idea of kissing Father's old setter.

At last Julie sobered and returned her gaze to the paintings. Her eyes rested methodically on one after the other in troubled concentration.

"It's too bad they don't have faces," she said at last. "They'd be real paintings if they just had faces."

As if drawn by a magnet, she approached the table where Cousin Ruby had set down her palette. Picking it up, Julie slipped her thumb into its opening and balanced it on her hand. She studied the little cups of bright color; then she reached out and seized the brush lying on the table.

"Julie!" gasped Elizabeth. "Julie, put those things down."

But Julie, if she heard, paid no attention. Instead, she continued to hold the palette and brush while again with great attention she studied the paintings.

Ever since she had first seen them, a strange

urge had taken possession of Julie. These faceless paintings had the same effect on her that the blind eyes of statues always had. She longed to take a pencil and put pupils onto those blind eyes so that they could *see*. Now she felt compelled to provide these gorgeously gowned figures with features that would make them human beings at last. To her, for all their fine draperies and rich colors, they were simply nothing at all. They would continue forever being nothing at all until they were given faces.

It had long been recognized in the family that Julie had some talent for drawing, though nobody took it seriously. When they had their drawing lessons at school, doing China lilies in the spring and leaves in the fall, Julie's drawings were unquestionably the best. She had done portraits in pencil of most of the girls' dolls, and Elizabeth had considered these drawings good enough to keep. She had also made some quite exceptional sketches of Old Bess, the gray mare, which Fred had taken the pains to tack up in the barn. So now it was not completely out of character for Julie to be balancing a palette in one hand and holding a brush in the other. Though, of course, she had never before worked in oils.

"I don't want to know," said Elizabeth. "I don't want to know anything at all," and she hastened toward the sliding doors, parted them a very few inches, and edged her way into the back parlor.

Clara eyed her as she came in. "What's keeping Julie?" she asked in a low voice.

Elizabeth carefully avoided Clara's eyes and made believe she hadn't heard. When it came right down to it, she didn't know what Julie was doing. The last she had seen of her, she was simply standing in the middle of the front parlor looking at the paintings with a palette and a brush in her hands.

Uncle Aaron and Father had got into an argument over politics and the women folks were swapping recipes. Cousin Hester had heard about a new way of making strawberry jam. "You simply put it out in the sun without cooking it at all," she declared.

"I wouldn't want to risk all that sugar," said Mother.

"I should think the ants would get into it," said Clara.

"You put it on the roof," explained Cousin Hester.

Clara sniffed. "Who does?"

"I intend to," said Cousin Hester crisply. "I shall simply crawl through my bedroom window onto that little balcony over the bay window and set the pans up above the eaves."

"Everybody to his taste," said Mother pleasantly. "I think I'll stick to the kitchen range."

"I'd welcome anything that freed me from a hot

kitchen at this season," said Cousin Hester, looking over Mother's head.

"There's something in that, all right," Mother agreed, but you could tell she had no intention of making strawberry jam on the roof. Not ever. So they changed the subject and began talking about fall styles. And now Cousin Ruby began to take part in the conversation.

After a while it was time to go.

"Where's Julie?" asked Mother.

"In the parlor," answered Elizabeth, "looking at the paintings."

Mother parted the sliding doors and called between them, "Julie, dear, it's time to say good-by." She hesitated, then opened the doors wider. "Julie," she said sharply. Then she let out a cry.

In two quick strides Father was through the doors and into the front parlor. "What's wrong, Alice?"

But Mother didn't have to answer. All the women, including Elizabeth, had crowded into the parlor after Father. Only Uncle Aaron was left in his chair in the bay window. Julie was nowhere around and the reason for her disappearance was plain to see on every painting. Each painting now had a face. No longer were they blanks. True, the features and expressions of these faces somewhat belied the elegance of the attire, but the overall effect had brought a dimension to the canvasses which they had previously lacked. Now the figures had character.

There was a light to each eye and a quirk to each mouth which might have been the peculiarity of the artist's style. Or it might have defined the narrow limits of her genius. Whatever the reason, each face wore an expression of raucous joviality which, combined with the elaborate costumes, had succeeded in changing Cousin Ruby's careful works of art into very funny pictures indeed.

Despite Mother's real despair, Father began to laugh. One look from Mother choked off his mirth, however. But Father's hearty outburst had been enough to pique Uncle Aaron's interest. In another moment he had eased himself out of his chair and made his slow way into the opening to the front parlor. The little crowd gathered there drew back to let him in. He stood quietly for a moment, looking intently at the paintings, and then he flung his head back in what could only be described as a howl of joy. For the first time in her life Elizabeth beheld the underside of Uncle Aaron's chin. She saw also the little gold collar button that held his shirt collar fastened. Then Uncle Aaron lowered his head almost to his middle while his right foot beat a thumping tattoo on the rose-covered carpeting of the front parlor. He was gasping and wheez-

ing now, and Father stepped to him and seized his elbow.

"Uncle Aaron," he said, giving the old man a shake. "Get hold of yourself. This isn't good for you."

Uncle Aaron reached carefully around and hauled a large blue bandanna handkerchief from

his hip pocket. "Good for me!" he repeated between wheezes. "This'll keep me going for another
year." Tears had spilled out his eyes and over his
bony cheeks, losing themselves in his whiskers. He
wiped his eyes and trumpeted once into the blue
bandanna before restoring it to its pocket. Slowly
he wheeled around to Cousin Ruby. "Don't you
touch those," he said to her. Cousin Ruby started to
speak. "Don't you lay a hand on 'em. I want to look
at 'em every day." Deliberately he circled about
and started into the back parlor. "You and Renfrow
can make some new ones. If you want," he added.

A few minutes later, Julie, curled in a corner of
the back seat of the Peerless, watched her family
come out of Uncle Aaron's house and through the
gate in the picket fence, and up to the car. Her
face was wet with tears, and the hem of her dress
was crumpled from wiping them away.

Father went at once to her side of the car,
opened the back door, and looked in at her. She
returned his gaze miserably.

"I don't pretend to understand what prompted
you to do anything so terrible," he said. "Do you
know you made it possible for Uncle Aaron actually to laugh at your Cousin Ruby's paintings?
Can you imagine how she felt?"

Julie nodded.

The others had got into the car. Mother was
looking over the front seat, first at Father and then

at Julie. Clara and Elizabeth sat rigidly, looking straight ahead.

There was a long silence and then Father said, "Get out and go right now and apologize to Ruby. Take your time. We'll wait."

Without a word, Mother reached a handkerchief to Julie, who got down out of the car and walked resolutely up to the house. She twisted the doorbell and heard it jangle faintly from within. Then there were steps along the hall and the door was opened.

"I want to speak to Cousin Ruby, please," said Julie in a small voice to Cousin Hester, who had again gone to "see who it was."

"Come in," said Cousin Hester, looking faintly surprised.

Julie stepped into the long hall and the front door was closed behind her. She watched while Cousin Hester's tall figure with its flapping skirt hem disappeared into the back parlor. She tried to think of how to frame her apology. "Please forgive me, I didn't mean to do it," she tried over in her mind. But that wouldn't be right, because she *had* meant to do it. She had wanted to do it, because she had wanted to give those poor figures faces. Perhaps "Please forgive me" would be enough.

In just a moment a light appeared at the other end of the hall and Cousin Ruby was hurrying toward her. But this was like no Cousin Ruby Julie had ever seen. Her eyes were bright, almost luminous, her cheeks were flushed, and she was *smiling*. Straight to Julie she came and when she was within reach of her and before Julie could say a single word, Cousin Ruby dropped onto one knee and gathered the little girl into her arms. At this Julie dissolved into tears, burying her face on Cousin Ruby's starched shoulder.

"There, there," murmured Cousin Ruby into Julie's ear, "there, there." She patted her gently on the back. "The old paintings weren't really good anyway. And I can make new ones." She held Julie at arm's length while she applied Mother's hanky to her eyes and nose. "You really shouldn't have done it, of course. And you must promise, Julie, never, never to do such a thing again. But you know something?" Julie looked into her eyes, a question in her own. "I'm really glad you gave them faces. You wouldn't understand, of course. But, Julie, I'm really glad. So don't you feel bad about it any more."

Nothing was said when Julie got back into the car. On the way home, Mother relayed some family news that Aunt Harriet had given her and Father grumbled about Uncle Aaron's political opinions. The old boy was getting senile, he thought, and Clara sniffed at this.

When they came in sight of the elderberry bush, Father flung a question to Julie over his shoulder.

"What did Ruby say when you begged her pardon?"

"She said she was glad I had done it," Julie answered.

Clara sniffed very loudly and Father and Mother exchanged quick, amused glances.

"Well, don't ever do it again," Father told her, turning the car into the driveway.

"I won't," promised Julie.

With that promise the events which had clouded this visit to Uncle Aaron were forgiven and could now be forgotten. Father never held a grudge, nor did he ever remind a faulty child of past mistakes.

"Sufficient unto the day is the evil thereof" was his favorite and most frequent quotation.

But two years later, when Uncle Aaron finally died and his will was read, that visit was startlingly and most unexpectedly brought to mind. A codicil had been added to the will, dated the day following that fateful visit, and it read:

To Elizabeth Allen, for gallantly saving the pride of an old man, five thousand dollars.

To Julie Allen, for giving me the best laugh of my ninety years, five thousand dollars.

The money came in handy when, many years later, the girls started to college.

As for Cousin Ruby, she and Mr. Renfrow were married two months after that will was read. Julie and Elizabeth were often invited to their house to spend the night, and always went joyfully. Cousin Ruby let Elizabeth make cookies, and Mr. Renfrow, who was now Cousin Hugh, showed Julie how to draw.

Cousin Hester and Aunt Harriet went on living in the house with the bay window in the back parlor. The Allens went rather often to see them, but Julie and Elizabeth found the visits always sad and disappointing. They missed the presence of Uncle Aaron in the window. Even though you couldn't really like him, still there was something special about a person past ninety who had a long white beard and growled!

4

Mr. Whipple

School had started, and here they were right in the middle of the harvest!

It isn't fair, thought Julie.

Why did school have to start now when her help was needed? This year for the first time, Julie had been allowed to drive Old Bess and Blackie between the orchard rows as they pulled the flat-bed truck from one stack of prune-filled lug boxes to the next. It was a little irritating that Old Bess always seemed to know exactly where to stop even before Julie did. But at least Julie was there, her feet swinging just above the singletrees, to get her going again. Fred, who paced beside the truck and swung the heavy boxes onto it at each stop, assured Julie that he didn't know how he had managed last summer without her, and rejoiced that she was now nine years old and capable of handling the team. So the start of school had come as a more than usually resented intrusion upon her activities.

She voiced her impatience to Mother in a tone bordering on impudence.

"I don't see why I can't stay out if the Russo kids can." The Russo family came each year to pick the prune crop. Since the fruit, when ripe, fell from the trees to the ground, all but the very youngest of the children could help with the job, and did.

Mother, in no mood for argument this morning, snapped back her reply. "Their father needs their wages and your father doesn't need yours. That's why."

"Will the Russos go to school when the prune picking is over?" inquired Elizabeth hastily. She knew the answer to that as well as anybody, but hoped to ease a dangerous moment.

"Of course," said Mother, putting their breakfast down in front of them. "Put your dishes in the sink when you've finished. I'm going out to the grader."

And out she went, leaving Julie and Elizabeth to eat their breakfast all alone in a silent dining room. For Father and Clara were already out at the grader, dipping the freshly picked prunes and spreading them on the trays.

It was going to be another hot day, a regular scorcher. Why can't school wait until it gets cooler?

thought Julie, swallowing her Grape-nuts and cream.

Father and Fred had long been at work, Fred bringing the boxes of prunes up from the orchard and Father lighting a fire under the dipper. Before the prunes were shaken down through the grader and spread on the long trays awaiting them, they were first dipped in a hot preservative liquid. Father did the dipping, lowering and hoisting the big sieve, then spilling the prunes out onto the grader by means of a long handle attached to the sieve. Onto the grader they spilled and were shaken down to the trays at the end of the grader. The gasoline engine that ran the grader made such noise under the roof of the open shed that conversation had to be shouted back and forth between the two extra "hands" Father had hired for the harvest and Mother and Clara working at the trays. When a tray was filled, the two men carried it out to place it in its row on the drying ground, an open area bordering the county road between the driveway and the elderberry bush.

Julie loved the harvest time with all its bustle and excitement, especially this year when she was permitted to handle the team and the flat-bed truck. She hadn't even minded when the weather turned hot, because it was good weather for drying prunes and she had a rancher's tolerance for it. But now all this was changed. No longer were her services considered necessary. Now she would have to trudge through the heat to the first day of school. It never once entered her head that anyone would take the time or trouble to drive her there. Only a major calamity could have got Father down from the dipping platform or Fred off the flat-bed truck. Julie and Elizabeth, like the other children, walked to school. It was unthinkable that children should do anything else, except in the very worst of the winter's storms.

This year the sisters were no longer in the same schoolroom. Julie had moved on into the fifth-grade room and Elizabeth now occupied Julie's old desk in Miss White's room. As before, Ethel Tucker sat across the aisle from her.

The summer had made a vast difference in Ethel. Now she looked very much like all the other girls. Her blond hair was neatly braided in two pigtails which were joined at about the region of her shoulder blades in a neat ribbon bow. She had shoes on her feet, and her cheeks were filled out.

As good as her word, Mother had informed the Grange ladies of the family in the shack beside the blacksmith shop. Immediately, food and clothing and bedding had found their way there. Before the summer vacation had fairly begun, Mr. Tucker had been offered a job on the Mosher ranch and had moved his family into the decent little cottage on the edge of the orchard near the county road.

Later, after a business call on Mr. Mosher, Father was able to report that Mr. Tucker had married and brought a new mother home to his children. From the looks of Ethel this first day of school, Elizabeth decided she was a good mother. Now the baby could stay at home all the time, and no longer would little Chester have to sleep on two chairs in the cloakroom.

The day wore on with little profit to anybody. It was just too hot for study. Elizabeth's wrists stuck to the paper when she practiced her handwriting, and Herman Dilling, at the blackboard, was able to erase his whole arithmetic problem with the flat of his hand.

At last, along in the afternoon, Miss White told them to put their books away, and devoted what was left of the school day to reading aloud.

On the long walk home, Julie and Elizabeth stopped to rest in the shade of the big black-walnut trees lining each side of the road in front of the Raley place. Seating themselves on their lunch boxes, they wiped their faces with the hems of their dresses.

"Gosh, it's hot," said Julie.

Elizabeth agreed, remembering that they still had half a mile to go. Just now it seemed a very long way.

Suddenly, both got to their feet. Around a bend in the road behind them came a horse and buggy which they recognized at once. The horse was a big bay and was throwing his feet in a way peculiar to Mr. Whipple's fine pacer.

As one, they picked up their lunch boxes and waited.

The shiny open buggy with its bright red wheels was almost past them before its brooding occupant noticed the two expectant figures at the roadside. Instantly, he pulled up the horse and cranked the buggy over so that they could get between the wheels.

"Didn't notice you," Mr. Whipple apologized. "Get in."

The girls clambered up onto the seat beside him without a moment's hesitation, for they were allowed to ride with anyone they knew. Glad as they were for the lift, they would have let Mr. Whipple drive past without a word. One didn't beg a ride.

He made sure they were safely seated before speaking gently to the big bay horse. Then they were rolling along smoothly and quietly on the rubber tires, the breeze of their speed cooling their moist faces.

Mr. Whipple was a figure of some mystery in their part of the countryside. He lived in the biggest house anywhere around and drove the best horses. He had no wife, but hired a housekeeper to cook and clean for him. Not one of the Grange ladies had ever been invited to his house, though several of them, including Mother and Clara, had dropped in for a chat with Tina when they went to pick berries. Mr. Whipple had the finest blackberries in the neighborhood and his neighbors were always welcome to them. It was thought that he kept a good deal of money in his house because he paid his men's wages in cash. But whatever the cash he kept on hand, it might not have seemed so very much to Mr. Whipple, for he was a well-to-do man. Everyone stood in a little awe of him, everyone, that is, except Father, who was probably the nearest thing to a friend Mr. Whipple could claim among his neighbors.

Always, whenever Julie and Elizabeth had caught a ride with him, Mr. Whipple voiced a remark which they found unbearably funny. The fact that he repeated it each time only made it funnier. Now, as usual, they waited to hear it, praying not to disgrace themselves when it came.

Sure enough. Just as they got to the elderberry bush, Mr. Whipple swung his head around and said solemnly, "This is the happiest time of your lives."

Immediately Julie and Elizabeth swelled up like a pair of toads, their lips pressed tight and their faces turning crimson as they fought to hold back their laughter. For it would be rude to laugh at a grownup, especially when he had been kind to you.

The happiest time, indeed! How could any

grownup be so foolish? Didn't they have to go to school? Didn't they have to do whatever their parents decided they must, whether they wanted to or not? Could they hitch up a fine bay pacer to a buggy with shiny red wheels and go driving about the countryside any old time they felt like it? The happiest time! They thought Mr. Whipple, for all his money and all his kindness, must be a rather stupid man to entertain such ideas.

He stopped the buggy in front of the driveway and cranked the wheels again to let the girls out.

"Remember me to your parents," he said formally when they had spoken their thank-yous. Then he lifted his hat as high as if they had been grown ladies, spoke to the big bay horse, and drove away.

There was no one to greet them when they toiled up the back stairs and entered the kitchen. They went all through the downstairs rooms, calling, before they remembered that of course Mother and Clara would be out at the grader working. So they climbed upstairs and changed into their play clothes, and then went out to the grader too.

That evening there was cold roast beef, potato salad, and stewed tomatoes for dinner, with fresh strawberries and cream for dessert.

"I don't want any salad and I don't want any tomatoes," announced Julie, sliding into her chair. "Just meat."

Father, who was serving, laid down the meat fork and stared at Julie in honest surprise. "Do my old ears deceive me," he demanded, "or did I actually hear you say you didn't choose to eat the food your mother has set before you?"

Julie dropped her head. "I don't like potato salad and stewed tomatoes," she mumbled.

Father sent his glance down the center of the table to Mother, who was serving the stewed tomatoes into sauce dishes. She met his eyes, her own troubled.

"What's got into you, Julie?" she asked, continuing to dish up tomatoes. "You've always eaten them before."

Something had got into Julie, all right. It had taken possession of her as soon as she woke up that morning and it had grown in her all day. Perhaps it was the extreme heat that made her feel irritable. Perhaps it was the sight of the lucky Russos not having to go to school, not yet anyway. Perhaps it was not finding anybody in the house when she came home from school. Perhaps it was because everybody was busy at something which didn't concern her in the least. Perhaps, even, it had been that foolish remark of Mr. Whipple's. Anyway, by suppertime, Julie felt cross as two sticks and there wasn't a thing she could do about it. That is, there wasn't until she decided she wanted only meat for dinner.

"You'll eat your salad and your vegetables or you won't eat anything," declared Father.

Julie gave him one quick look, saw that he meant every word of it, and promptly rose from her chair. In horror, Elizabeth saw her stalk from the dining room, and started to go after her.

"Stay right where you are," said Father, so Elizabeth settled back. But she couldn't eat. She couldn't swallow a thing. Not even the stewed tomatoes. So pretty soon she said, "Excuse me, please," to Mother and escaped.

Julie wasn't anywhere around. Elizabeth even climbed up into the hayloft to look for her. Coming out from the barn into the sunset light, she paused to look off toward the hills beyond Mr. Whipple's place. Their gently sloping sides, brown at this season, were now pink in the light of the fiery sunset flaming up from behind the Santa Cruz mountains on the other side of the wide valley. Even the house had changed from white to pink. Fascinated, Elizabeth stretched out an arm and marveled to find that it, too, had taken color from the sunset's glow.

But she must find Julie.

She rounded the barn and started into the orchard, following the little road that led to the pumping plant. The Russo family was camping there, because the pumping plant was conveniently located in the middle of the orchard and had water piped to it. Before she reached the camp, Elizabeth could see the bright light of the Russo campfire. And then she saw something else which stopped her dead in her tracks. Sitting in a ring of Russos with a plate on her lap and her dark bangs shining in the light from the fire, was Julie. Elizabeth studied the scene for several seconds before turning resolutely around and returning the way she had come. There were some things it was better not to know too much about. And her one concern had now been taken care of. Julie would not go to bed supperless.

Back at the house, she found Clara and Mother clearing away the supper things. Father was filling his pipe. Elizabeth tried to get through the kitchen unnoticed, but without success.

Father eyed her, shook out his match, and puffed once before asking, "What happened to Julie?"

Elizabeth hesitated long enough to try out several answers before realizing that only one was possible.

"She's with the Russos," she said.

Father thought this over, puffing calmly, while without comment Mother and Clara went about their kitchen chores.

"Eating with them?" asked Father.

Elizabeth nodded miserably.

At last Father said, "It's a lot more comfortable eating outside than inside these nights. Can't say I blame her much."

But Mother looked displeased. "I don't like one of my children imposing on the Russos," she said. "This mustn't happen again."

"It won't," Father assured her. "Julie was just making the most of an opportunity. Come on, Betts, let's stroll down and get her."

So Elizabeth, with her hand in Father's, went down the back steps and through the orchard toward the Russo camp to find Julie and make peace. Fanny wagged faithfully behind them, her tongue lolling. Even now, with the sun gone, the evening was uncomfortably warm.

Later, Mother saw to it that Elizabeth would not go supperless to bed either. And as Julie watched her sister's plate being filled, she decided that maybe she'd have some potato salad after all. And some meat. What was left of the stewed tomatoes was by this time cold, and no one, not even Father at his most cantankerous, would expect a person to eat cold stewed tomatoes.

While Father and Mother and Clara sat on the front-porch steps trying to get cool in the sickly little breeze wandering down from the Alviso marsh ten miles away, the sisters ate their belated supper. Then they washed and dried their dishes.

For a while they sat in the darkening twilight with their elders, listening to talk of prunes and prices and plans for the coming winter. And then it was time to go to bed.

All the tired household was thankfully asleep when, shortly after midnight, its peace was shattered by the telephone ringing in the kitchen downstairs. Julie and Elizabeth sat bolt upright from their pillows, their hearts pounding. Tensely they listened as they counted the rings. One, two, three —pause. One, two, three—again. It was their ring! What could it mean? Something awful must have happened; why else would anyone be calling them at this time of night?

They heard Father come out of their parents' bedroom and hurry downstairs as the phone kept up its more or less steady clamor. At last it ceased, and with every door in the house wide open they plainly heard Father's "Hello!" There was a moment's silence and then Father exclaimed, "My God!" Now Mother came out of the bedroom and hurried down to join Father, calling as she went, "Harry, what is it?"

Almost immediately, Clara came into the girls' room, a lighted lamp in her hand. Electricity hadn't been put into the house yet, though that was one of the plans for the winter if the prune prices held up.

"It's probably your Uncle Aaron," she informed the girls, whose eyes, wide and questioning, were fastened on her. "We've been expecting it for a long time."

But Julie shook her head. "Father wouldn't have said 'My God' if it had been Uncle Aaron," she declared.

"And you mustn't say it, either," returned Clara.

"Something awful has happened," Elizabeth said and she began to whimper.

Clara set the lamp down on the dresser and went to sit beside Elizabeth on the bed. "We are all here together," she said quietly.

In a few minutes, they heard Father and Mother coming back upstairs. Straight down the hall to the girls' room they came, and then stood together at the foot of their double bed.

Father did the talking.

"That was Tina calling from Mr. Whipple's place. She wants your mother and me to get over there right away. Mr. Whipple has been badly hurt."

"How?" asked Julie.

Father hesitated for just a moment and then he said, "Tina isn't quite sure just how. His head is hurt and Tina has sent for the doctor. But she wants us there with her until he comes, so of course we're going."

The girls nodded.

"Clara, may we speak with you for a moment?" Father asked. Clara rose and followed them out of the room.

So Julie and Elizabeth knew right away that Father was holding something back which he was about to tell Clara. Something had happened to Mr. Whipple, something so bad that it couldn't be told in full to two little girls in the middle of the night. They looked at each other for a long, shocked moment, then slid down into bed. But not before they had reached for the tossed off coverings, which, despite the warm night, they pulled up tight to their chins.

It was thus that Clara found them when she came back into their room. "Trying to smother yourselves to death?" she asked, looking down into the two pairs of frightened eyes staring up at her from the pillows. Gently she reached down, took hold of the bedclothes, and started to draw them toward the foot.

"Please leave the sheet, Clara," begged Elizabeth. "I'm not so scared with something over me."

Clara left her the sheet. "There's nothing to be afraid of," she said. "People get hurt every day."

"In the middle of the night?" asked Julie, and Clara sniffed.

They listened as Father backed the Peerless out of the garage and drove down the driveway. In the stillness of the autumn night, they could hear its motor for a long while. But at last it faded away, and now they felt truly abandoned. Father and Mother were both gone in the middle of the night! But of course they still had Clara. Timid Clara!

Suddenly, below the window of the bedroom, they heard heavy steps coming up the back stairs. Then someone pounded loudly on the back door.

This was too much for the girls' taut nerves and they sprang out of bed. But Clara was her usual calm self.

"It's somebody we know," she told them, "else Fanny would have barked."

She started out of the room with Julie and Elizabeth at her heels. Clara had taken up the lamp and they had no wish to be alone in the dark.

Clara led them down the stairs, their shadows huge and black in the bobbing light of the coal-oil lamp. She called through the window to the screen porch, "Who is it?"

A voice beyond the screen door answered, "It's Russo."

Clara at once unlocked the kitchen door and went out onto the screen porch. Then she unhooked the screen door and opened it to Mr. Russo.

"I heard the automobile go out and I thought maybe somebody he's sick. Maybe something I can do, or my wife."

"You are very kind, Mr. Russo," said Clara, "but

everything is all right here. One of our neighbors has been badly hurt, and Mr. and Mrs. Allen have gone to him."

Mr. Russo's black mustache cast a heavy shadow across his face in the soft light, making him look brigandish. But his eyes, dark and earnest, belied the fearsome mustache. His presence here in their behalf was all the proof anyone needed that Mr. Russo was among the kindest of men. He was also one of the bravest, for he had forsaken his own land of no opportunity to find his fortune in a newer country whose language he couldn't speak and whose ways were foreign to him. Here he had staked his future and that of his children. And though their only livelihood was the work they could find during the harvest season, with occasional odd jobs during the winter months, still the Russos were happy and hopeful.

Now he looked at the two little girls, barefooted and in their nightgowns behind the tall woman holding the lamp. His face was still troubled.

"How your friend get hurt?" he asked.

"We won't really know until Mr. Allen gets back," said Clara.

Mr. Russo laughed, showing white teeth under the black mustache. "Funny time to get hurt. He fall out of bed?"

Clara smiled politely at the joke. "It does seem a

little mysterious," she allowed. "But whatever they discover, it won't have anything to do with us. So we can all just return to bed. And thank you for coming, Mr. Russo. It was very thoughtful."

"That okay," said Mr. Russo, starting down the steps. Then he turned to look up at them. "Remember. You need somebody, you call."

"I'll remember," said Clara, and the three went back into the kitchen and Clara locked the kitchen door again.

But Clara had been dead wrong. What had happened at Mr. Whipple's had real concern for the three waiting in the tall white house on the edge of the county road.

Hardly had they gone back upstairs when Fanny began barking furiously. But it wasn't her usual "There-is-somebody-here-you'd-better-know-about" bark; it had a savage edge, as if she were saying "Get out."

The three exchanged startled, frightened glances and then Clara said, "You two get back into bed and stay there." She set the lamp on the dresser. "I'm going downstairs."

"In the dark?" asked Elizabeth, a quaver in her voice.

"Why don't you call Mr. Russo?" asked Julie. "He hasn't had time to get back to their camp yet."

"If he can't hear Fanny, then he couldn't hear me," said Clara, who had to raise her voice to be heard above the dog's barking.

Later they learned from Mr. Russo what had taken place below their windows.

Mr. Russo had almost reached the corner of the barn on his return to his own family when Fanny, who was wagging after him across the back yard, let out a roar and raced ahead into the orchard beyond the barn. What was she after? he wondered, quickening his steps.

It was when he had got almost to the pumping plant and the white tent in which his family slept showed faintly through the darkness that he saw a shadow like a detached bit of the night slip into the engine house. Right behind it came Fanny. She didn't follow the shadow inside, but stood at the door barking fiercely. Suddenly she whirled, almost knocking into Mr. Russo, and tore around to the side of the building. Running after her, Mr. Russo rounded the engine house in time to see the shadow of a man come out the side door, the very door Father had dashed out of when the "Indians" had surrounded him. Fanny let out another fearful roar and was off in pursuit. Seconds later, Mr. Russo heard a man's yell above the dog's barking. Had she bitten him?

By now the whole Russo family was out of the tent, demanding to know what was the matter.

Mrs. Russo had the baby pressed tight in her arms.

"Tony," shouted Mr. Russo to his eldest child, "run up to the house and tell Miss Allen to get the sheriff. Run now!"

Tony ran.

Clara and the two girls were huddling anxiously in the kitchen when Tony padded up the back steps. His pounding on the screen door brought the three out onto the back porch.

"My father says 'Get the sheriff,'" he panted, his thin chest heaving under his nightshirt. They could still hear Fanny barking from deep in the orchard.

"Come in, Tony, while I phone," said Clara, and Tony came in.

There wasn't much she could tell the sheriff except that the family dog was acting strangely, that there had been a bad happening in their neighborhood only a little while before, and that this might have some connection with it.

She listened without comment as the sheriff replied, and the three children stood around her, their eyes never leaving her face. At last she said, "I understand. Thank you," and hung up.

"The sheriff says that two men in a runabout are already checking all the ranches between Mr. Whipple's and town. I'm afraid you'll have to know that a young man tried to kill Mr. Whipple tonight. They believe that he is trying to escape through

the orchards to the railroad yards in town where he can jump a freight. We're directly in his line of march if that's what he intends to do. Fanny may well have him treed by now. Let's hope so."

"Will he hurt Fanny?" asked Julie.

"The sheriff says he isn't armed. He tried to kill Mr. Whipple with a hatchet. When Tina heard Mr. Whipple scream, she went to him as fast as she could and found a candle which the man had dropped snuffed out in the bedclothes, and the hatchet beside it. Evidently he intended to rob Mr. Whipple after killing him."

"Will Mr. Whipple get well?" asked Elizabeth.

"We don't know yet," said Clara. "He is very badly injured."

Just then they heard a car come down the driveway. It stopped and Clara picked up the coal-oil lamp and went out onto the back porch, the children following her.

Two men came up the back steps and onto the porch. They wore cowboy hats and boots and guns slung low on their hips.

"We're from the sheriff's office, ma'am," the taller one said to Clara. "We'd like to search the place."

"There's no one in the house," said Clara, "but our dog may have the man you're looking for down in the orchard." She turned to the three huddled in the kitchen doorway. "Tony, take these men to your father. And tell your mother that if she feels nervous, she is welcome to bring her family back here for what is left of the night."

So Tony, walking with great pride despite the nightshirt, led the two towering deputies down the back steps and into the darkness. Right then, Julie would have given anything in the world to have been Tony Russo. Fanny was still barking.

In a remarkably short time, the taller deputy was again standing on the back porch. "We got him, ma'am," he said to Clara. "That's a real great dog you got there. She'd already bit him in the leg before he climbed into a prune tree. And she wouldn't let him come down out of there. Every time he made a move to get down, she went for him. He told us."

"It's all so dreadful," said Clara distressfully. "I hate to think of Fanny's biting anybody."

The deputy moved toward the screen door, his face troubled. "I don't like to think of nobody getting hit over the head while he's lyin' asleep in his own bed, neither," he said.

Clara nodded. "Of course you're right. I suppose," she added dubiously.

"And another thing," the deputy continued, holding the screen door ajar, "this here kid tried to kill a man who'd befriended him. He was livin' in the

house and treated like a son. How's that for grati-
tude?"

Clara sighed. "It's hard to understand."

"Well, good night, ma'am. I'm goin' after the
Black Maria now. My pardner's holdin' a gun on
the prisoner. It's all okay now. Be glad you got that
dog." The deputy clattered down the back steps. In
another moment they heard the runabout drive
away.

Nothing of that night seemed "okay" to the three
waiting for the return of Father and Mother. A
neighbor had been almost murdered in his bed; he
might even now be dead for all they knew. And a
young boy whose life was over no matter how long
he might live was being held a prisoner in their
own orchard.

Clara glanced at the kitchen clock.

"Half past two. I think I'll call the Whipple place
and tell them about the boy. They might be worried that he will come back and do more harm.
Because of course he must be crazy."

The girls listened as Clara gave the number to
the operator and the call went through.

Father himself answered the phone, for Clara's
first words were, "Harry! I'm glad it's you."

She described briefly what had happened, giving
Fanny full credit for the capture. Then she hung
up and turned to Julie and Elizabeth.

"Your father and mother are staying on with Tina until full daylight. She's pretty upset. Mr. Whipple has gone to the hospital in the ambulance. The doctor thinks he will live. So let's go back to bed and try to sleep."

She spoke so casually that Julie and Elizabeth did go back to bed and to sleep. It was wonderful that anyone as timid as Clara could make you feel, all at once, perfectly safe.

One day after the rains had started, Mr. Whipple came driving into the Allen back yard in a buckboard drawn by a quick-stepping team. Julie and Elizabeth were out in the yard to greet him.

"I'll call my father," said Julie as soon as he had stopped.

"I've come to see you and your sister," said Mr. Whipple, and the two girls looked astonished. What could Mr. Whipple want of them?

"I have something for you," he added, getting down from the buckboard. "Back here."

The girls stepped up to the back of the buckboard to see what might be lying there. What they did see was too amazing for speech. Two brandnew girls' bicycles lay flat on the bed of the buckboard! And they were full size. One was red, the other blue.

"Now you won't have to walk to school anymore," said Mr. Whipple.

Father, hearing voices, came out of the garage where he had been tinkering with the magneto.

"What's going on here?" he called out gaily as he approached the little group at the buckboard.

"Look," Julie said, her eyes never leaving her father's face. "Look what Mr. Whipple has brought us."

There was silence while Father soberly contemplated the two bicycles, and Julie and Elizabeth forgot to breathe.

This was a handsome present, especially from a near-stranger. Would Father allow it? There had been talk of bicycles if the prune prices held up, and while this had been pleasantly exciting, they knew all the needed things would have to come first. But now, here, as by a miracle, were the bicycles. Would Father let them stay?

"I'm not sure I can let you do this, Mr. Whipple," Father said at last. "It's very kind of you to want to, but I'm not sure . . ."

Mr. Whipple cleared his throat and began speaking as if he were selecting every word with utmost care.

"You can't prevent a person from saying 'Thank you,' Mr. Allen," he began. "I can never thank you and Mrs. Allen enough for your great kindness to me and Tina on that dreadful night. And then, the way you managed my harvest as well as your own while I was recuperating. These bicycles are a very small token of my appreciation for all you've done."

He finished speaking and Father didn't say anything for a moment. Then he looked up at Mr. Whipple, nodded, and the two men shook hands briefly. Next Father reached over the side of the buckboard.

"Who gets the red one?" he asked.

"Julie," said Elizabeth promptly. "Julie prefers red."

So Father lifted out the red one first and Julie stepped up quickly and laid her hands on the handle bars. Next, out came the blue one and Elizabeth seized hold of it. Then they turned to Mr. Whipple.

"Thank you very much," they chorused just as they always had whenever he stopped to give them a lift.

And just as always, Mr. Whipple lifted his hat high as he said, "I hope you will enjoy them. This is the happiest time of your lives."

For once, the words seemed not the least bit funny. Hearing them now, Julie and Elizabeth looked at one another and then back to Mr. Whipple, their faces sober. Could Mr. Whipple, after all, be right?

"Do you know how to ride 'em?" asked Father, smiling broadly.

"Yes," said Julie. "We've practiced on Alberta's bike at school."

"Then off you go," said Father.

"How far?" asked Elizabeth.

"To the elderberry bush and back."

5

Mother Goes to Town

Julie was waiting near the kitchen stove for Mother to hand her down the bucket of warm mash for the hens. November was here with its crisp mornings, so now Julie had an added Saturday chore.

Across the kitchen, Clara was washing the lamp chimneys in fresh clean suds and Elizabeth was drying and polishing them. Her hands were just the right size to squeeze up into the lamp chimneys, so this was her Saturday chore.

She looked long-faced and sullen this morning as she dragged the dish towel round and round inside each chimney, not at all her usual self. Since this was Saturday, the Allens were going to town—all except Clara and Elizabeth. Elizabeth had missed school yesterday because of a cold in her head and

Mother had decided she had better stay in another day. And Clara, despite Mother's protests, had insisted on being the one to stay home with Elizabeth. So, even though Clara had promised to make taffy to pull, Elizabeth was far from happy.

Going to town was usually the most exciting event of the week, though its pattern never varied.

First, there was the stop at The Farmers' Union to unload the bucket of eggs and to pick up the next week's groceries. Mother's hens laid so well even during the cold weather that she always had a surplus beyond what the family could use.

After the visit to The Farmers' Union, Father drove to the post office, which was centrally located. There he parked the Peerless and they all got out, the ladies heading straight for Hill's, the largest department store in town. No one ever knew just exactly where Father went, and he never asked anyone to join him.

Julie and Elizabeth loved to go to Hill's. You could find almost anything there and the clerks were friendly. While Mother and Clara selected dress goods along with buttons and thread to match, or a few yards of elastic, or some other article necessary to their modest wardrobes, Julie and Elizabeth strolled importantly between the aisles, playing they were grown ladies and deciding on all the lovely things they would have when the wished-for day actually came. Tiring of this game (and Julie tired of it rather quickly), they got Mother's permission to visit the basement, where the saddles and toys were kept. There the sisters parted, Elizabeth going to the doll counter and Julie making a beeline for the far corner of the basement where the fine fragrance of new leather became more enticing with every step she took.

Not even Elizabeth knew Julie intended to be a cowgirl when she grew up. All the while she was pretending to be a grand lady among the yard goods upstairs, her heart was with the saddles. They were as familiar to her as old friends. And when occasionally she found one missing, for of course the saddles were there to be sold, she tried to imagine where it had gone and what the horse that now wore it looked like. Once a good-natured clerk, having observed the loving way she was stroking the saddle on the display rack, lifted her up and set her squarely astride it; Julie sat there until Mother and Clara came to claim her. That had been a Saturday to remember!

Having quit Hill's at last, the four would saunter slowly along First Street just looking in the windows. Whenever they came to a window with shoes in it, they had to pause for several minutes while Mother and Clara memorized its contents in order to compare that store with the next one. Just twice a year they entered a shoe store, once at the start of summer and once in the middle of fall. So they had to be very careful to know their minds before purchasing.

Sometimes, strolling in this way, they would come upon Father, chatting on a street corner with a friend he had run into. Then they knew there would be plenty of time to "do" the other side of First Street before returning to the Peerless. But no matter how leisurely they were, they nearly always got to the car ahead of Father. Sometimes they waited so long for him that Mother grew impatient. But when at last he did show up, he always had some highly important information about the probable price of prunes and the best advice on whether to hold or sell.

The last stop was always the library. Father carried the books in and put them on the librarian's desk. Then he marched down the long room to the magazine section. Here he lost himself in *Popular Mechanics* until Mother was ready to go. He was quite willing to let her pick out his own books for him, as she knew his tastes as well as he did, and could always remember what he had read. The children's department was in the basement, down a twisting iron stairway. Julie and Elizabeth never lost any time getting down there, for the rule for children was one book to a card, and choosing wisely required time. A week's reading could be ruined by a hurried choice. This Saturday Elizabeth would have to depend on either Julie or

Mother to select her book. But she would not need to feel concern on this score since both were good pickers.

Julie edged closer to the kitchen range as she saw Mother take hold of the galvanized bucket containing the mash. She lifted it off, lowered it carefully, and slid the pail over Julie's reaching hands.

"Be careful Fanny doesn't upset you on the back steps," she said.

This had not happened yet, but Mother mentioned it every time Julie took the mash out. It didn't happen this morning, either. Julie managed the back steps without difficulty and staggered through the kitchen garden and out into the big open back yard, the bucket hitting halfway between her knee and ankle. Midway across the yard, she set the bucket down and lifted her face to the sky. Clouds were scudding above the Whipple hills to the south. It looked like rain. Starting off again, Julie was thankful that Father never stayed home on account of rain.

She reached the henyard without spilling a drop, and began pouring the thick, slow-moving mash into the waiting trough. She tried not to hit the backs of the crowding hens, but a few of the greediest got splashed.

Her chore accomplished, Julie rinsed out the bucket at the henyard tap and returned it to its own special place on the back porch so Mother wouldn't have to hunt for it the next morning. Then she went upstairs to change her clothes for town.

Since Father didn't have to go to the bank that day, they would not be leaving until after lunch. This meal was apt to be sketchy on Saturdays, but on this Saturday, with Clara staying home, it was almost like dinner. There was a bubbly, brown-crusted baking dish of macaroni and cheese, a platter heaped with slices of cold roast beef, and devil's-food cake for dessert. Only salad was lacking. Macaroni and cheese was Elizabeth's favorite dish and Clara had made it specially for her out of sympathy. But she only toyed with the good food on her plate, holding her fork listlessly. You couldn't really blame her. Missing a trip to town was enough to take away anyone's appetite.

At last Mother pushed back her chair and rose. "I expect, Harry, we'd better be on our way," she said to Father. "That is, if you've finished."

"I have," said Father, folding his napkin, then carefully rolling it and stuffing it into its napkin ring. Julie was hastily doing the same. "Just let me light my pipe and I'll go out and start the car."

"We'll get our hats on," said Mother. "Come, Julie."

"Be sure and take the eggs," said Clara as Father started into the kitchen. "They're in that bucket by the back door."

Mother and Julie soon reappeared with their hats on. "Are you sure you don't want to go in my place, Clara?" Mother said.

"Yes," said Clara, "I'm sure. This will give me a chance to put the hem in my black skirt."

"Good-by, dear," said Mother, kissing Elizabeth, who immediately burst into tears right there at the dining-room table.

"Why, Elizabeth!" exclaimed Mother. "You're sicker than I thought. I wonder if you shouldn't have a dose of castor oil."

At once, Elizabeth's head jerked up from her elbow. She sniffed loudly, gave her eyes a swift dab with her napkin, and declared herself to be "all right." But Mother continued to study her with concern, and noticing her worried look, Elizabeth began seizing soiled dishes right and left and hurried with them into the kitchen to show Mother how little there was wrong with her.

Julie, with a casual "So long," went through the kitchen with her arms full of books. By the time she reached the garage, Father had put the eggs in the Peerless and was about to begin cranking the car. Julie climbed up and unloaded the books onto the back seat. From there she watched admiringly as Father started to crank, his head bobbing above the brass radiator band on each turn he gave the heavy engine. When all his effort failed to get a response from under the big hood, he let go of the

crank and came back to fiddle with a small knob
mounted on the steering wheel. Then he patiently
returned to the front of the car and, puffing now,
spun the engine again. This time it gave off a faint
report, a kind of halfhearted sputtering noise. Like
a flash he dropped the crank and raced around the
front fender to the steering wheel. Just as his hand
was about to close on the knob there the engine
ceased its sputtering and a dismal silence settled
over the garage. Father muttered something under
his breath and returned to the crank.

This time there was no sound at all out of the
Peerless, and after several spins Father let go of the
crank to lean panting against the radiator. He
spoke to Julie over the top of the hood.

"You'd better wait inside the house, Julie. Tell
your mother there'll be a slight delay."

Julie got down from the back seat and left the
garage to Father and the Peerless. She caught
Mother just as she was coming down the back
steps, her gloves on and her handbag over her
arm.

"Father says there'll be a slight delay. The car
hasn't started yet," she informed Mother.

Without a word Mother turned and re-entered
the back porch with Julie behind her.

Julie began to feel anxious as she waited with
the others in the dining room for the engine roar
that would signal Father's victory over the mag-

neto. Would she, like Elizabeth, miss the trip to town? Of course Mother would go even though the magneto should triumph over them, for she would drive Old Bess in the buggy. But in that event would Mother decide to take Julie with her? Or Clara? Father didn't figure in her concern as he had never yet gone into town behind Old Bess and it was perfectly understood that he never would. And with Father at home, there was no longer any need for Clara to stay with Elizabeth.

Suddenly, in the midst of Julie's speculations, there came the stamp of hurrying feet up the back steps and through the kitchen, and Father burst into the dining room, sweat running down his face and his hat pushed back from his forehead. His eyes were very dark, his face flushed, and his breathing that of a runner at the end of his stretch.

"It's no use, Alice," he panted. "That magneto isn't working again and I've got to take it down. I've told Fred to hitch up the buggy. You'll have to go in behind Old Bess."

Mother rose and picked up her handbag. Very quietly she said, "That's all right, Harry, though I'm disappointed we can't go together. As for Old Bess, it isn't the first time I've gone into town behind her, and it probably won't be the last." She turned to Julie, who waited tensely. "Come, dear," she said, and without further delay or confusion, they again took leave of Clara and Elizabeth while

Father went upstairs to change into his old clothes.

Julie helped Fred pull the buggy out of the carriage section of the barn, each taking a thill. Mother stowed the library books and the eggs in the back of it while Fred went to get Old Bess. Presently he reappeared, leading the mare, traces dangling. Old Bess was hanging back, stretching her head out as far as it would go, making him drag her toward the buggy.

Hauling her around, Fred cocked an eye at the sky and said jauntily, "Looks like you're goin' to get rained on before you get back."

"Then you'd better put the top up," Mother said.

He lined up Old Bess with the thills before replying.

"It won't go up," he said.

"Why not?" demanded Mother.

"I tried to put it up just now, but one of the struts is broke. Must of broke when I put it down two weeks ago Sunday."

Fred was allowed now and then to borrow Old Bess and the buggy when the mare wasn't working.

Mother made an impatient sound and turned to Julie. "Run and get the umbrella. You know where it's hanging on the back porch."

Julie ran, found the umbrella, and returned. Fred was fastening the traces and Mother had climbed into the buggy. Julie handed up the umbrella before climbing up herself.

"Thank you, dear," said Mother, taking it. "If it does rain, you'll simply have to hold this over us. If it weren't for those eggs and the library books, I'd stay home."

They were ready to go now. Fred straightened the reins along Old Bess's back and placed them in Mother's hands while Julie climbed up into the seat and tucked her end of the lap robe under her. Mother handed her the umbrella, then clucked hopefully to Old Bess.

One never could predict how Old Bess might respond to any given signal. She acknowledged Mother's by swinging her head around for a long steady look at what she was hitched to. Satisfied at last, she swung her head front again, shook it, and sneezed. Next, she took a slow step forward, and without further prompting, started willingly across the yard. By the time they were halfway down the drive, she was moving at a brisk trot which continued past the elderberry bush and almost to Orchard School. There, she began to slow up.

"I didn't think she'd keep that pace for long," Mother said resignedly.

"I've never seen her trot like that before," said Julie. "I wonder what's wrong with her?"

"Search me," said Mother, "but I'm grateful for small favors."

Mother perfectly realized that Old Bess was no more eager to be driven to town than Mother was to drive her. She was, of course, a plow horse doubling as a buggy horse, but she had not the slightest enthusiasm for either role. All she wanted was to be let alone, going and coming from corral to barn as her appetite and the weather moved her. All her life she had resisted work with every bit of horse sense at her command, and she commanded a lot.

Her best trick was to pretend genuine effort while actually avoiding it altogether. As Fred described it, there they would be, going along without a hitch, the team pulling smoothly, the plow almost singing through the ground with the dark soil sliding evenly off the share, when, without warning, Old Bess would step over the traces. Of course this would necessitate a full stop until Fred could work her back into position again. And then when they came to the end of the furrow, Old Bess would behave as if suddenly struck blind. Groping her way around and into the next line of march, she acted as if she hadn't the slightest notion of where she was going or what was expected of her when she got there. Fred could yank and yell till the orchard rang. Old Bess would stumble helplessly about, making this moment when the plow was out of the ground last as long as she could.

Blackie, the other half of the team, was as tractable and willing as Old Bess was crafty and lazy. He would pull his heart out if you let him. Why, then, didn't Mother prefer Blackie to Old Bess on those Saturdays when the magneto failed them? The answer was simple—Blackie wouldn't quite fit between the buggy thills and Old Bess just barely did.

Before he got the Peerless, Father had had a buggy horse almost as fine as Mr. Whipple's. Father's father had given him that horse on his twenty-first birthday and it had drawn the buggy the first time Father had taken Mother for a drive. Only, of course, she wasn't Mother then. And it was a good many years before she was. But during all that long time after she and Father were married and before Julie and Elizabeth came along, Dandy was a source of great pride to Father and a delight to Mother, who was a very good horse-woman.

Three years ago it had become clear that Dandy should be retired to pasture. He had served the Allens long and well and deserved his rest. So Father spoke to Mr. Whipple about turning Dandy onto the hill range where several of the aging Whipple horses were enjoying decent care and leisure, and Mr. Whipple had been quite willing to let Dandy join them. Mother, though regretting Dandy's departure, was sensibly keeping a shrewd eye out for any likely bit of horseflesh. One day,

soon after Father's talk with Mr. Whipple, she reported that one of the Grange ladies was willing to
sell her four-year-old gelding. Mother knew the
horse and said she considered it sound and a bargain at the price.

"No horse is a bargain today at any price,"
Father said with considerable warmth. "Not a
buggy horse, that is."

Mother looked at him in astonishment. "What
will we do without a buggy horse?" she asked.

"We'll have an automobile," replied Father.

That was the first Mother knew about it. A few
days later Father drove the Peerless home, and
Dandy was led away to the Whipple hills.

Now, while Mother waited for the self-starters
which Father confidently assured her would be
coming along "first thing you know," she was
forced to put up with Old Bess.

They jogged past Orchard School, going slower
and slower. By the time they reached the blacksmith shop they were moving hardly faster than a
walk. Mother clucked and slapped with the reins,
all to no purpose. It seemed as if Old Bess was
making a prodigious effort. Her big ironshod feet
pounded the hard dirt of the road, and her wide
rump heaved heavily up and down. But still the
buggy went at a snail's pace. This gait was her
special buggy trick.

When they had slowed to a point where something drastic had to be done, Mother reached for the whip. It was then she noticed that the whip socket on the dashboard was empty.

"That Fred!" she exclaimed. "He forgot to put in the whip."

Julie looked around quickly. "What'll we do?"

"We will have to accept the situation," Mother declared. "We are at the mercy of Old Bess. And she knows it."

Julie said nothing, though she fully understood that Mother needed the whip, not to punish Old Bess for her laziness, but merely to remind her that the possibility of punishment was at hand. Only a brute whipped a horse, and if ever Fred had taken a whip into the orchard with the team, he would have been fired at once. A buggy whip was purely for emergency, like the spare tire strapped to the back of the Peerless. Just to tickle Old Bess with the braided string tip of the whip was enough to remind her of her duty and to encourage her to do better.

Mother sighed and settled back against the seat. "I'll bet she knew right from the start that I didn't have a whip. That's why she went so well at first. She didn't want me to have to use it until we had gone too far to turn back for it."

"Can't you buy one at The Farmers' Union?" Julie asked.

"Certainly I can," Mother returned. "But I don't

see myself spending two dollars and fifty cents for a whip when we already have one. What on earth would we do with two? Besides, she'll go better when we turn toward home."

Julie nodded, recognizing the wisdom of Mother's words. Two dollars and fifty cents would buy a pair of shoes each for her and Elizabeth. It would pay for a doctor's visit if they needed one. And it would keep Father in pipe tobacco for a very long time.

The afternoon was well advanced by the time they pulled up in front of The Farmers' Union. Mother headed Old Bess into the curb and handed the reins to Julie.

"I won't be a minute," she said, getting down from the buggy. She lifted out the bucket of eggs and disappeared into the store without a backward look.

She had nothing to worry about. Old Bess would stand indefinitely and nothing frightened her. It was her only good feature as a buggy horse. Relaxing one hip, her head hanging below her chest, Old Bess would doze until a determined tug on the reins forced her awake.

Julie hoped Mother would take her time. She knew that today they would not be going to Hill's. Old Bess had taken care of that. So part of today's fun would be in watching the people going and coming along Santa Clara Street and feeling at one with the Saturday shoppers. There was still the library to look forward to, but she knew that visit would be a hurried one. So far it hadn't rained, but the sky was lowering and any moment it could start.

Julie had waved to two people she knew before Mother emerged from the store, her arms full of paper bags. A man wearing a clerk's apron walked just behind her, similarly burdened. Carefully the two stowed the week's groceries in the back of the buggy. Then Mother got in with the clerk's courteous help, took the reins from Julie's hands, and backed Old Bess, stumbling with sleep, away from the curb. She had barely got the buggy straightened around when over the sounds of the street came a frantic-sounding *clang! clang!* The ambulance! Julie glanced over her shoulder and gasped. It was coming straight toward them at a furious speed. Old Bess and the buggy were squarely in its path.

"Mother," cried Julie, really frightened, "Mother, *do* something. It's going to run right over us."

Mother was doing what she could. Again and again she jerked on the reins, calling, "Get up!" But Old Bess was in no mood to hurry. The gong had not unsettled her in the least, though its clamor was enough to wake the dead in Oak Hill Cemetery two miles away.

Again Julie looked back over the folded-down

buggy top and this time her frightened eyes met the angry stare of two men on the front seat of the ambulance. It was that close behind the buggy! Fortunately it had halted its wild speed in time, and they seemed in no imminent danger of being run down. The gong was still sounding madly and everyone on the block had stopped to watch the interesting tableau of the barely moving buggy and the ignominiously stalled ambulance. For it couldn't get around Old Bess because of the on-coming traffic, and Mother couldn't pull Old Bess over to the curb because other vehicles were already parked there. All she could do was get to the intersection as quickly as possible and then pull over to let the ambulance by.

At last, desperate, Mother reached over and seized the umbrella from Julie's inattentive hands. Leaning well over the dashboard, she brought it down with a hard smack on Old Bess's ample rump. Startled, the mare awoke fully, snorted, and lunged forward, jerking the buggy almost off the pavement. Behind them, the ambulance started up with a noisy grinding of gears, closely following the buggy into the intersection. There it roared past them, but not before a white-jacketed man leaned from the front seat to yell at Mother over the top of the gears and the gong, "Madam, you should always make way for the ambulance!"

"Was that the ambulance that came for Mr.

Whipple?" Julie asked when again the street had returned to normal.

They were clumping east toward San Fernando Street and the library, having turned clear around in the intersection. Mother seemed not to have heard Julie's question, so she repeated it.

"The same," replied Mother, her face unnaturally pink, and that was all the talk there was the whole way to the library.

It was when they were coming out of the library with their arms full of books that it began to rain. It was just a drop here and a drop there at first. But before they could reach the buggy where Old Bess was tied to a hitching post, the drops quickened. Hurrying, they succeeded in stowing their precious cargo safely under the buggy seat, unhitched the mare, and scrambled up themselves before the clouds really opened. Julie hastily shook out the umbrella and held it over them. But since the rain was from the south and they were traveling in that direction, it was necessary to tilt the umbrella in order to keep the rain off. This obscured Mother's view of the street, but for once Old Bess's horse sense came in handy. She could be counted on to keep to her side of the street.

Everything went well, including Old Bess, who knew she was headed home, until they came to Second Street. Here Mother pulled up to let a streetcar pass. Old Bess, disliking the rain in her face and impatient to get home, seemed to resent the pause and even fought the bit in a quite spirited way. The streetcar had barely rattled past before she started up, despite all Mother could do to hold her back. Straight in behind the streetcar she swung, and with characteristic awkwardness, slammed one big ironclad foot smack down on the wet steel rail. What followed happened so fast that Julie had trouble trying to sort it all out when later that evening she tried to explain it to Elizabeth. No sooner did Old Bess hit that rail than she stopped dead, her four feet sliding out from under her. At the same moment a tremor passed through her and her tail rose, like a fountain, every hair distinct. For a moment it held there, appliquéd against the rain. Then slowly, the tail fell and Old Bess gathered her feet under her. Next, she was off and running.

"Hang on, Julie," cried Mother. "Never mind the umbrella. Hang on with both hands. Old Bess is running away."

This had become clear to Julie before ever Mother spoke. She needed no second warning but sent the umbrella soaring with a backward fling. Then she grabbed the buggy rail with one hand and clutched onto Mother with the other. Rain smarted against her eyes but she dared not take them off Old Bess, who seemed flattened out in the thills as with head extended she raced along. Just what had happened to her at the moment when her big hoof met the rain-wet streetcar rail, Julie didn't really know. But plainly something had, and Old Bess was either frightened by it to the point of running away, or else she was only eager to get out

of that vicinity as quickly as possible. There seemed a kind of reason in the way she ran, or maybe they were being saved from collision by the quick thinking of other people in the street, who guided their vehicles out of the way of the oncoming buggy.

Julie stole a look at Mother. She was holding the reins taut in strong hands. Her head was tipped down a bit to allow her hat brim to keep some of the rain out of her eyes. And to her daughter's astonishment, a thin, grim little smile curled the corners of her mouth. Julie began to feel somewhat reassured as she remembered that, according to Father, Mother had never lost her head in any emergency, not even when the chimney caught on fire. Now Julie could see that she was actually driving Old Bess, though she couldn't stop her, and so far she had managed to keep the buggy wheels away from the streetcar tracks.

Twice, men darted from the curb in an attempt to stop the runaway, but both times Old Bess managed to evade them. Fortunately Second Avenue ran on to the end of town and there was little to fear at intersections, for the clamor of her hoofbeats was an effective klaxon.

On they went until the business section had been left behind and houses lined the street. Now and then Julie caught sight of a startled face at a front window and a few children ran down front steps to stand on the sidewalk looking after them despite the rain. If only Old Bess kept on a straight course as she had thus far, and didn't try to free herself of the buggy by banging into a tree, or try to turn suddenly into a side street, if only these two dangers could be avoided, they would be safe. For Old Bess couldn't keep this pace for long.

They passed the turn they should have taken for home and it was then that Old Bess began to slow perceptibly. Almost, thought Julie, it was as if she suddenly realized that she had missed the turn. Suppose she had recognized it and had cut the corner into it? They might both have been killed, for the buggy would surely have been turned over.

Yes, Old Bess was slowing down. Mother eased up on the reins a very little and let her run on until they were beyond the houses and the orchards had begun. When at last the mare was going at something near her normal gait, Mother gently pulled her down to a walk and guided her off the road to a quiet stop. She turned to Julie.

"Are you all right, dear?"

Julie, not quite up to speech yet, nodded.

Silently the two sat there watching the heaving sides of Old Bess and listening to the rain on the fallen leaves of the orchard beside them. The mare's head hung low and she seemed utterly spent.

"Here," said Mother, passing the reins to Julie.

She got down from the buggy and went to the mare's head. Julie could hear her murmuring soothingly as she passed her gloved hand down Old Bess's nose. Then, patting her affectionately on the neck, Mother got back into the buggy and tucked the lap robe around her.

"Put your hat on," she said to Julie.

It was only then that Julie realized her hat had blown off and was hanging down her back by the elastic under her chin. She hauled it on even though her head was sopping.

"We'll wait until Old Bess has her wind back," said Mother. "Then we'll let her go home at her own speed even if she *walks* every inch of the way." She leaned across to tuck the lap robe more securely around Julie. "Whatever failings Old Bess may have, we will always owe her a lot after today. Any other horse would have taken that turn for home and killed us both. Thank goodness Old Bess has horse sense."

It was almost dark when at last they turned into the driveway at home. Old Bess had walked a good part of the way and of course both Mother and Julie were soaked to the skin. Lights had been lit in the house and both Father and Fred were out in the yard watching the road for them.

"What made you so late?" demanded Father in the irritated tone of one who has been badly worried and then finds his worries over, and needless.

He handed Mother down from the buggy at the same time that Fred swung Julie down in a wide arc that sailed her legs out.

"I'll tell you all about it when we get inside, Harry," said Mother in a perfectly calm voice. She turned to Fred. "I'm going to fix a warm mash for Old Bess and please rub her down carefully. She's had a hard day." To Father she added, "As long as I live, I shall never drive Old Bess or any other horse to town again."

And she never did. Even for Mother, the horse-and-buggy days were over.

6

Father Makes Christmas

Christmas was far and away the most exciting event in the whole year for Julie and Elizabeth, but not for the reasons which make this true for other children. The festival was heightened and enlivened for them because Father still believed in Santa Claus. Preposterous as it seemed, there could be no doubt about it, for he actually disliked "the old cuss," as he always referred to Santa, and you had to believe in anything you didn't like. It wouldn't make sense otherwise.

Of course, Julie and Elizabeth had once believed in Santa, too. Then they had started to school and their belief ended. But for Father, Santa Claus con-

tinued to be real, and there were times as Christmas neared and Father's feud with "the old cuss"
quickened its pace, there were times when Julie
and Elizabeth *almost* went back to believing.

Christmas started for them right after Thanksgiv-
ing, and it usually started in the same way. One
night they would be upstairs undressing for bed
when, for just an instant, Santa's face would appear
at the bedroom window over the back-porch stairs
where the ash maple was. The face never stayed
for more than a moment, and though they stood
frozen in an entanglement of long underwear, staring at the window, it never reappeared. Not that
night, anyway. And when a bit later they lay snuggled in their bed, doubt about their own disbelief
in Santa Claus would not be downed. Just suppos-
ing, they speculated, this really was Santa Claus
come to check up. It was then that they reminded
each other of some forgotten chore, or the spat
they had had on the way home from school. It was
part of the tradition that Santa was generous only
to good boys and girls. Or so Father would con-
stantly assure them from this night until Christmas
Eve. But then a pleasant surge of excitement
would go over them, bringing a grin to their faces
as they lay staring up at the high ceiling in the
dark. The fun had begun; Christmas had begun.
The days could only get better and better as they
ran on.

This year it happened exactly as it had before. It was Elizabeth who first spied the whiskered face at the window.

"*Santy Claus!*" she shrieked.

Julie, hopping about in an effort to shed her long flannelette drawers, swung around just in time to see the ruddy countenance vanish back into the night. Frantically she hauled at her underclothing as she hobbled toward the window. As usual, she arrived too late to see anything. By the time she had got the window open, whoever was responsible for getting Santa's face up there had gone. She carefully studied the ash maple, but it loomed darkly between the back porch and the tank house, and there was no moon. She hung out the window and shivered in the cold while she watched the tree, only halfway hoping to see the shadow of a man's body among its bare branches.

"Julie!" said a voice behind her, and she hastily drew back into the room and shut the window. Mother had come to tuck them in. "What on earth did you think you saw out there?" she demanded.

"I didn't see anything," Julie said, smiling a bit foolishly. "But just seconds ago, Santa Claus was looking in this window. It had to be Father. And if I could catch him out, I could prove to him how silly it is for him to pretend to believe in Santa. You can't believe in something you're pretending."

"How do you know it isn't Fred?" asked Mother.

"How do you know it isn't really and truly Santa?" asked Elizabeth.

"Now, Elizabeth, you cut that out," said Julie. "It's bad enough to have Father acting like a child."

"But I *am* a child," Elizabeth reminded her stoutly. "And I want to *be* a child. And I'm glad Father believes in Santa Claus. I wish I believed in him too." And Elizabeth flung herself, wailing, into Mother's arms.

"There, there," said Mother comfortingly. "We all believe in the spirit of Christmas and Santa Claus is a symbol of that. So in a way we all do believe in him. Father just enjoys it all more than most people, I guess. There, there."

So Elizabeth dried her tears and crawled into bed and Mother tucked her in, then came around to the other side and tucked in Julie. Then she heard their prayers. After that, she kissed them good night, took up the lamp, and went away.

The sisters snuggled against each other.

"I'm sorry I made you cry," said Julie.

"That's all right," said Elizabeth kindly. "I don't know what made me. I guess it was thinking about how awful it would be if Father didn't believe in Santa. We wouldn't have any fun at all."

There was a silence and then Julie said, "We sure wouldn't have as much fun. Maybe that's what grownups mean when they say that Christmas is for children. They stop believing in things that are fun."

For the second time a really serious doubt entered their hearts. It was like the curious apprehension they had felt with Mr. Whipple and the bicycles. Now Elizabeth voiced it.

"Maybe it isn't much fun to be a grownup after all."

Julie thought this over for a moment. "If you're the right kind of a grownup, like Father, then it wouldn't be so bad."

"No, it wouldn't," agreed Elizabeth. "And we have to go on helping him to be the right kind of grownup."

"Like pretending to believe in Santa Claus?" asked Julie.

"Yes," said Elizabeth. She raised herself on one elbow to look toward Julie in the dark. "And you know something, Julie? If we practice pretending now with Father, why, when we have our own children we can be the right kind of grownups for them."

"You may be right," said Julie soberly, and on that conclusion, they fell asleep.

The next morning at breakfast, they reported what they had seen at their bedroom window the night before.

Father dropped the soupspoon with which he had been eating his oatmeal and half rose from his

chair. He cast a furious glance around the breakfast table and said in an awful voice, "Has that old
cuss started hanging around here already?"

His only answer was Clara's sniff.

When at last he left the table, a change had
come over him. He seemed preoccupied, brooding,
like a man threatened. As the days went by and
other appearances of Santa were reported, the
change in Father deepened. Everyone noticed it. A
scowl settled between his eyes. Like the twin
ravens of Odin, apprehension seemed to perch on
one of his shoulders and suspicion on the other. He
was seen to glance up at the roof whenever he
crossed the back yard, and several times when he
sat, moodily looking into space with Julie and Elizabeth secretly observing him, he allowed his pipe
to go out.

One evening just a week before Christmas, they
came upon him sitting in front of the living-room
fire with his blue-black Smith and Wesson six-
shooter lying across his knees.

They stared in unbelief. He had never gone this
far before.

"What are you doing?" demanded Julie.

Without taking his eyes off the glowing coals,
Father answered darkly, "I'm wrestling with my
conscience."

"You mean you're planning to shoot Santy
Claus?" cried Elizabeth.

"I haven't got around to any plans yet," Father informed her. "The idea has just taken hold of me and I like it."

Elizabeth rushed forward and flung herself between his knees, knocking the gun aside. "Father, you wouldn't! You mustn't! You couldn't do anything so mean."

"Yes, I could," replied Father. "That old cuss is vying for my children's loyalties and affection and I'm not putting up with it any longer."

Julie grinned. "Have you got a silver bullet, Father? Santa Claus is magic; it will take a silver bullet to get him."

Father looked up, amazed. "You don't say! Well, of course that settles it, for I have no silver bullet. I'll just have to think of something else."

Stooping sadly, a picture of utter dejection, he left the room, the six-shooter dangling from a listless hand, and they knew he was returning it to the top bureau drawer in his bedroom where it would remain forgotten as it had until this evening.

From that night forth, Father was a shadowed man. Julie and Elizabeth kept a watchful eye on him, for Christmas vacation had begun and he was hardly ever out of their sight. Suppose he actually should try to shoot Santa? And what would he think up next?

"Maybe we should take the gun out of the bureau drawer and hide it," suggested Julie.

"*Julie,*" gasped Elizabeth. "How could you even think of such a thing? You know we aren't allowed to touch that gun even when Father's there. And to go into his bureau drawer . . ." Elizabeth let the sentence trail away unfinished. The idea was too shocking for speech.

"I guess you're right," said Julie quickly. "I didn't really mean it. But he's worse this year than ever before. He seems to get worse as we get older. What will he be like when we start to high school?"

"He'll be lots older then, too," said Elizabeth sagely. "Maybe by that time he won't believe in Santa either."

They contemplated this awful possibility for a moment and then Julie said slowly, "We'll be different, too, by then."

Elizabeth pondered this, and then said firmly, "Maybe you will be, but I won't. I'm not ever going to change. Even when I'm grown up I'm going to be me, Elizabeth." She looked into Julie's eyes, her own beseeching. "Please don't ever change, Julie. Promise me you won't."

And Julie promised easily.

On the evening of December 23, they came upon Father sneaking noisily through the kitchen, gun in hand. So he was determined to shoot Santa, silver bullet or no silver bullet.

As one, they fell upon him, Elizabeth clasping him around the knees while Julie tried to pull down the long arm brandishing the gun aloft.

"I saw him, I saw him!" yelled Father in a voice that bounced along the kitchen ceiling and slid down the walls to rattle the milk pans drying on top of the kitchen range. "I saw the old cuss. Up on the roof I saw him."

Julie and Elizabeth added their shouts to his, creating such bedlam that Mother hurried into the kitchen to take a hand in it. "Put that gun away and behave yourself, Harry," she scolded Father in a tone she hadn't used with Julie or Elizabeth in at least two years. "They'll be so excited they won't ever go to sleep."

So Father let the girls win and stalked off with the gun, his shoulders sagging.

The next night was Christmas Eve. This was the night Santa always came for a visit and he had been appearing regularly each year even though the sisters no longer believed in him. Or did they by Christmas Eve? One thing they were sure of—it wouldn't really be Christmas Eve without him.

And it was on this night while the dishes were being washed that Father made his last great effort to thwart "the old cuss."

This time, when Julie and Elizabeth discovered him again sneaking through the kitchen, gun in

hand, though they struggled manfully to hold him, Father broke away and ran from the kitchen, the two girls in hot pursuit.

Gaining the center of the back yard, he looked wildly up at the roof and fired twice. Slowly he lowered the smoking gun while Julie and Elizabeth stood tense with pleasurable terror, and the moonlight flooded everything.

"Were those silver bullets?" queried Elizabeth.

"Blanks," replied Father, his eyes still earnestly searching the roof. "But I missed him. I missed the old cuss."

Elizabeth sniffled, but Julie spoke up, her vicarious knowledge of the Old West being greater than her sister's.

"How could you 'miss' him with blanks?" she asked.

"The same way you could hit him with a silver bullet," returned Father, and Elizabeth stopped sniffling to smile shakily. It was all a little like finding oneself inside one of Father's Amazon stories. Still a question loomed large in her mind. Had Father frightened Santa away?

But no. Shortly after the dinner dishes were washed and dried and put away, Father was called to the house of the orchard bordering on the Allen place, just beyond the elderberry bush.

Julie and Elizabeth exchanged knowing glances. This was exactly the way it happened every year. And they had always thought how fortunate it was that Father happened to be called away about the time Santa was due to visit them. This visit was important not only for its wonder and excitement but because no matter what desirable things might be waiting for them under the Christmas tree tomorrow morning, nothing would compare to the gift which Santa would present to each of them on Christmas Eve. For as long as they could remember, their very special present had been handed to them by "the old cuss" himself on Christmas Eve.

Julie and Elizabeth seated themselves on the hearth rug, prepared to wait. Only one lamp glowed in the room where Mother and Clara sat reading. Off in a dark corner, the Christmas tree gave out a woodsy fragrance. It would remain untrimmed until after the girls had gone to bed to burst upon them as the crowning surprise of Christmas morning. The clock on the mantel ticked gravely and with a jerky rhythm which seemed to say, "Scared away; scared away."

Had Santa finally been scared away this year? Would this be the year that marked a change in Christmas? Julie was ten now, Elizabeth almost nine. Had the years scared Santa away? Sometime they would, of course; perhaps next year. But not tonight. Please not tonight, they both prayed as they listened to the seconds ticking by and waited for the sound of the front doorbell. Santa always came to the front door.

Suddenly, there it was, a peculiar clanging suggesting Christmas bells.

"I wonder who that can be?" said Mother, putting aside her book. Clara sniffed.

The girls got to their feet in an ecstacy of relief and anticipation.

"Come right in, Santa," they could hear Mother saying out in the hall.

Then the door to the hall opened and Mother came into the room followed by a tall figure wearing a long white beard and a heavy coat belted around a fat middle. In the dim light they could see black rubber boots below the coat. A round hat not unlike Mother's fur turban, always referred to by Father as "the Daniel Boone hat," was crushed down almost to his bushy white eyebrows. In the half-light it was impossible to tell the color of his eyes, which seemed strangely sunken beneath those bristling brows. This was Santa Claus, *their* Santa Claus. And if he bore small resemblance to the "official" Santa Claus installed in the heart of Hill's department store, he was infinitely more authentic.

He greeted the two women in a quavering voice, then turned his full attention to the waiting children, profferring his hand to each. Gravely they shook it, finding it authentically cold. And doubtless, fur hats were fur hats from here to the North Pole.

"Have you been good girls this year?" he asked.

"Pretty good," said Julie.

"We tried," said Elizabeth.

Mother spoke up. "I wouldn't trade them for any other two girls in the world, Santa."

"That settles it," said Santa. "You should know."

He began reaching into the pockets of the long coat. "I have something for you," he quavered, drawing out two small packages. Julie and Elizabeth took them shyly.

"May we open them now?" asked Elizabeth.

Santa gave a quick look around. "I saw your father walking up the road just before I came in. When will he be back?"

"I think there'll be time to open the packages, Santa," Mother assured him.

So there in the firelight they opened their packages. Julie found a red coral necklace in hers and Elizabeth had a little gold locket in the shape of a heart on a gold chain. Her name was engraved diagonally across the locket.

"Thank you, Santa," they cried. "Thank you."

"I'm glad you like them," said Santa. "And now I'd best be moving along. Your father may come back any minute and I have a long way to go tonight."

He shook hands again and started away.

"You'll be back again next year, won't you?" asked Elizabeth.

Santa paused and looked long at them both.

"I'm afraid not," he said sadly. "You're big girls

now. This is the last time for you." Noting their stricken faces, he hurried on. "But I'll be around. And one of these days when you have some children of your own, I'll be back. You'll see me then."

So Santa Claus went slowly from the room for the last time and Mother let him out the front door and into the moonlight. Julie and Elizabeth stood silent upon the hearth rug, the firelight soft about them, their special presents in their hands, and the certain knowledge in their hearts that Christmas would never be quite the same again.

For some reason, Father didn't return home immediately upon Santa's departure as he had in previous years.

"Perhaps he decided to take a walk in the moonlight," said Mother.

The girls went up to bed without showing him the wonderful gifts Santa Claus had brought them for his last visit.

At the breakfast table the next morning Julie wore her red coral necklace and Elizabeth her little gold locket.

Father leaned over to study each one carefully.

"Where did you get those?" he demanded.

"Santa brought them," said Julie.

"But he won't ever bring anything again," said Elizabeth, a slight catch in her voice.

"Well, if he won't, then I'll have to," declared

Father. "We're going to have Christmas, Santa or no Santa."

The words were warmly reassuring on this happy Christmas morning.

After breakfast came the tree, now closed off from them in the living room. Father opened the sliding doors and there it stood between two front windows, shimmering and beautiful above the packages wrapped in their white tissue, tied with red ribbon, and gay with Christmas stickers.

Some time after the tree came the Christmas dinner, followed by a long lazy time during which the light gradually faded out of the winter day, darkness crept from the corners of every room, and the candles on the Christmas tree were lit. This was the last year they would be using candles. Prune prices had held up well, and right after the New Year, Father was having electricity put into the house. Next year they would have tiny, electric tree lights like those they had seen at Hill's.

A grownup had to be in the living room with an eye on the tree every minute that the candles were burning. They could be dangerous, those candles, for at any moment one could gutter down and set a twig on fire. But their dancing lights were lovely and Julie and Elizabeth feasted their eyes on them this Christmas night, determined to remember them always.

"Aren't we going to have some carols?" asked Clara as they all stood in a half circle, admiring the gentle light on the tree. "I'll watch the candles."

Without a word, Mother went to the piano, spun the stool, then seated herself and struck a chord.

Behind her, Father reached an arm to Julie and Elizabeth, gathering them to him in a firm clasp. As their voices rose with Mother's, he suddenly joined his to theirs, singing out, gloriously off key:

"O come, all ye faithful . . ."